CW01459333

Karma, Reincarnation, and Past Lives

A Journey Through Time and Karma with
Real-Life Tales of Reincarnation

Joyce T.

© Copyright 2025 - All rights reserved.

The content contained within this book may not be reproduced, duplicated or transmitted without direct written permission from the author or the publisher.

Under no circumstances will any blame or legal responsibility be held against the publisher, or author, for any damages, reparation, or monetary loss due to the information contained within this book, either directly or indirectly.

Legal Notice:

This book is copyright protected. It is only for personal use. You cannot amend, distribute, sell, use, quote or paraphrase any part, or the content within this book, without the consent of the author or publisher.

Disclaimer Notice:

Please note the information contained within this document is for educational and entertainment purposes only. All effort has been executed to present accurate, up to date, reliable, complete information. No warranties of any kind are declared or implied. Readers acknowledge that the author is not engaged in the rendering of legal, financial, medical or professional advice. The content within this book has been derived from various sources. Please consult a licensed professional before attempting any techniques outlined in this book.

By reading this document, the reader agrees that under no circumstances is the author responsible for any losses, direct or indirect, that are incurred as a result of the use of the information contained within this document, including, but not limited to, errors, omissions, or inaccuracies.

Contents

Introduction   VII

    Crash Course

    Cockell and Sutton

    Varied Sources

    Relevance

    Overview

1. Understanding the Fundamentals of Karma   1

    The Law of Cause and Effect

    Karma in Different Cultures

    Karma Through Narrative

    Modern Practices

    Misconceptions About Karma

    Building Better Relationships

2. Reincarnation Explored   23

    The Cycle of Birth and Rebirth

    Historical Perspectives on Reincarnation

    Scientific Investigations

3. Real-Life Tales of Reincarnation   41

Children Remembering Past Lives

The Boy Who Lived Before

Consciousness and Memory

More Modern Tales of Reincarnation

Reincarnation Stories From Around the World

Reincarnation and Healing: Emotional Transformations

4. The Intersection of Karma and Reincarnation   67

Interconnected Journeys: Karma and Reincarnation

Past Lives Shaping Present Karma

Lessons From Past Lives: Practical Applications

Balancing Karma Across Lifetimes

5. Addressing Skepticism and Misunderstandings   87

The Skeptic's Guide to Reincarnation: Addressing Doubts

Scientific Perspectives: Evidence and Limitations

Cultural Misalignments: Bridging Eastern and Western Perspectives

Common Misunderstandings: Clarifying Key Concepts

Karma in Modern Context: Relevance Today

6. Practical Karma: Applying Teachings to Daily   107
Life

Mindful Actions: Creating Positive Karma

Meditation Techniques for Karmic Awareness

The Art of Letting Go: Releasing Negative Karma

Cultivating Compassion: Enhancing Karma

Everyday Karma: Simple Practices for Daily Life

7. Building Community and Spiritual Connection   129

Role of Sangha

Resources for Spiritual Growth

Interfaith Dialogue: Embracing Diverse Beliefs

Cultivating a Supportive Environment for Spiritual
Exploration

The Importance of Continuity in Spiritual Practice

Expanding Your Spiritual Journey Beyond This
Book

Conclusion   151

You and Me, We're the Same

Homestretch

Share Your Thoughts   157

Bonus Gift   159

References   161

Image References

Introduction

Karma isn't fate. Nor is it a punishment imposed on us by some external agent. We create our own karma. Karma is the result of the choices that we make every moment of every day. –Tulku Thondup

How can a vivid and complex life simply end? What comes after life? So many of us have chewed over this and asked about it. Maybe you've had bar discussions with your friends, partly drunk yet baring your soul about these fears.

A person could have a hundred dreams, a hundred friends, and a tight-knit family. They may be the kindest soul around, always ready to help others. But even the best of us can stop breathing with the slightest shift of luck. Let me tell you, I've pondered and panicked over this thought myself.

I believe you picked up this book because you have the same questions about death and what comes next that I did.

Crash Course

Karma

You may have witnessed or experienced the simplest form of karma. It is the philosophy that actions have consequences, but this idea can go deeper than that. Building on the law of cause and effect, karma goes several steps further and contemplates how our actions in this life and previous lives can decide our fate. It considers our indestructible soul, which goes through the cycle of life and death multiple times.

When I think of all beings on this planet having crossed paths regardless of time, distance, or even species, I find that the cosmos has offered us a gentle way of reconciling with death. This is why the concept of karma soothes me. We go beyond death to realize that life and the soul continue to thrive. This idea tells us that the universe, with its vast interconnectedness, operates on a principle of balance: What we give to the world in our actions will eventually come back to us, shaping our present existence and the experiences we will face in future lives.

Reincarnation

This is what I understand of reincarnation. It is the idea that after death, the consciousness is reborn in another body, thereby being revived with the thoughts and beliefs of the previous life. You may have heard consciousness being called an eternal soul that goes through multiple life cycles.

When we consider that we can and have lived many lives, rebirth and reincarnation can feel like part of our soul's cosmic journey. The idea of reincarnation becomes more than fanciful and becomes quite essential. It allows for a continuation of the soul's journey, offering the opportunity for growth and learning across several lifetimes.

Past Lives

Interconnected with the concept of reincarnation, your past lives may make themselves known through strange dreams, unexplained memories, and the sensations of déjà vu.

Many prefer to believe in tabula rasa, the idea that a newborn infant is a blank slate ready to absorb knowledge and experiences for the first time. But the thought behind past lives is that everyone may have lived before they were alive in their current body and that it is a matter of luck, focus, and fate that some of us can remember our previous existences.

Cockell and Sutton

For someone who believes in past lives, reincarnation is not merely a philosophical concept but a lived experience. Let's look at Jenny Cockell, a well-known figure who has researched her past life as Mary Sutton, an Irish woman who passed away 21 years before Cockell was born.

Cockell had vivid dreams of Mary Sutton's life in Dublin, Ireland, a place she had never visited before traveling there to verify the accounts. She recalled scenes before, during, and after Sutton's death, stating her consciousness had been separated from her body. Cockell even recounts how she, as Mary Sutton, watched others move around in the room after Mary's passing (Cockell, 1993). Cockell spent time and money tracking down Sutton's children, the oldest of whom was Sonny Sutton, a man who was astounded by the stranger's recollection of his mother's life.

Cockell has published books on her experiences and attended interviews, the latest being in 2017, when she recounted her experiences to Thanatos TV (Rohrbeck, 2017). Her frankness and positive attitude toward skepticism have encouraged people to come forward with unfamiliar memories and dreams of their own.

Every declaration is not without its skeptics. But we shall get to that further in the book. For now, I wish to explain how each life, with its trials and triumphs, can be seen as a chapter in the soul's journey toward wholeness. The idea that we are not limited to just this singular lifetime but that it is part of a much larger cosmic journey lends a sense of continuity and purpose to our existence. I find hope in this thought. Don't you?

Varied Sources

Many spiritual and religious traditions of the world believe in reincarnation, from Buddhism to ancient Greek culture and multiple indigenous communities across the globe. People have experienced and recorded case studies over the centuries, and some of the more powerful stories are of young children who recall their previous lives and even deaths. To the shock and amazement of people, some have been known to speak in the languages of countries they've never visited.

I will also present real-life instances, like that of Jenny Cockell, that professionals in the field have studied. Another notable example is the story of James Leininger, a young boy from the United States who, at a very early age, had detailed memories of being a World War II fighter pilot named James Huston Jr., who'd died in a plane crash. Another case involves a young girl from India, Shanti Devi, who vividly recollected her previous life as a woman named Lugdi Devi. The girl provided detailed information about her past family and home that was later confirmed.

It is stories such as these that reinforce how karma can certainly turn the tables around on us, as though the universe itself aches to address things left unfinished. Such true anecdotes prove that truth remains stranger and more beautiful than fiction. They show us the connection between karma and reincarnation and how the consequences of our actions across all our lives decide our destiny.

My aim is to ensure this book, *Karma, Reincarnation, and Past Lives: A Journey Through Time and Karma With Real-Life Tales of Reincarnation,* can help you reconcile with such a metaphysical concept and apply it to your life. We are used to having the world send us negativity in the form of global news, unfortunate luck, and natural disasters that are larger than life and out of any person's control. Amid all this, believing in karma and reincarnation might feel too optimistic and impractical. But, as substantiated by various cultures worldwide, acknowledging these philosophies might help realize that there is more to life than life itself.

Relevance

Perhaps you are a Buddhist or are familiar with the faith's teachings. You would thus be aware of *samsara* (or *saṃsāra*), the unending cycle of birth, life, death, and rebirth. This book will build on this understanding by exploring how the cycle of reincarnation is more than a spiritual idea. It can also help in matters of regular life where you can practice mindfulness, develop helpful meditative techniques, and otherwise strengthen your mind and body.

This form of clear awareness can significantly improve your mood and emotional balance by helping you stay focused in the moment. Meditation can help reduce stress and anxiety, as you're exercising your awareness of yourself and the environment you are in. Regular practice helps you observe thoughts and actions without judgment, which leads to greater emotional resilience and less overt physical reactions. Done well and consistently, your health can benefit from more stable cortisol levels and a stronger heart rate.

Overview

Let's have a quick chapter rundown of the topics we will cover in this book:

1. **Fundamentals of Karma:** We will explore the way karma presents itself in our existence and how we can rework our lives by incorporating this school of thought.

2. **Reincarnation Explored:** We shall discuss the unending yet varied explorations of lives as experienced by a single soul. This chapter will show how physical death need not stop consciousness from continuing to exist.

3. **Real-Life Reincarnation Tales:** We will read up on the documented cases of people who remember experiencing past lives and have had their memories verified by family, the public, and researchers.

4. **Karma and Reincarnation Interconnected:** This chapter will show us how karma and reincarnation are tethered and the ways they influence each other in our lives.

5. **Skepticism and Misunderstandings:** We will see how skeptics bring up valid and invalid reasoning to counter several stories. This helps us understand how true past-life memories can manifest and how these instances are relevant to us in the modern day.

6. **Practical Karma:** Here, we'll discuss the various ways believing in this form of cosmic karma is physically and emotionally beneficial to our lives.

7. **Building Community and Spiritual Connection:** We close the book after considering how the spiritual belief in karma, reincarnation, and past lives brings openness to our perception. This helps us broaden our minds and accept the diverse faiths of the world.

With an eager and open mind, you can find genuine inspiration and strength in the stories of people who can remember their past lives. If you can relate to these case studies, then I encourage you to feel empowered by your own experiences. Some memories can be devastating or inexplicable to witness and may leave you with more questions than answers, but you can break negative patterns, learn from your past lives, and improve your present situation. It is possible!

Join me on this journey as we explore what it means to truly embrace the concepts of karma, reincarnation, and past lives. My hope is that by examining these stories, I can shed light on the impact of reincarnation on human history. It helps shape the foundation of what it means to have a soul and what this soul is truly capable of. By exploring the widespread belief of karma across multiple lives, as we shall see in the following chapters, I will guide you to appreciate the interconnectedness of humans across time and space and past geographical boundaries and bygone eras.

Chapter 1

Understanding the Fundamentals of Karma

Belief in karma ought to make the life pure, strong, serene and glad. Only our own deeds can hinder us; only our own will can fetter us. –Annie Besant

We can trace the word "karma" to the Sanskrit root *kri*, meaning "to do" or "to act." It zeroes in on the actions we perform and the consequences they lead to, whether in this life or the next.

While not all faiths believe in multiple lives and reincarnation, the sentiment of reward and punishment is common and functions in varying ways. In some cases, it is closely related to the law of karma; in others, it is not. The prevalence of the theme, however, highlights that we like to believe we have a hand in what happens to us. It gives us a more active role in the unexplained happenings of the world, no matter how fair they may or may not be.

Across Religions

Different religions and sects interpret the philosophy of karma in their own ways. Many believe karma indicates that the magnitude of consequences is based on our actions across multiple lives. We can only break away from karma's outcomes altogether by escaping the reincarnation cycle and achieving liberation, or *moksha*, as seen in a few of these faiths.

Rooted in South Asian traditions, karma's definition changes across different religions and cultures. Faiths such as Hinduism, Buddhism, and Jainism understand karma through the reincarnation cycle, wherein a person's actions across multiple lives can result in consequences down the line. Abrahamic religions such as Judaism, Christianity, and Islam lean toward prioritizing the Day of Judgment as the only time believers receive answers and outcomes to their deeds.

Despite these varied interpretations, the central idea remains the same. Our thoughts, intentions, and actions can shape our lives and those of the people around us, thus determining everyone's future.

Relevance and Benefits

Karma can subtly manifest in our daily actions and decisions, often in ways we may not immediately recognize but which ultimately shape our experiences and the world around us.

For instance, a small act of kindness, like offering a word of encouragement to a colleague, can ripple out, fostering goodwill and co-operation in the workplace. Similarly, a decision to act with honesty, such as returning a lost wallet or admitting to a mistake at work, can build trust and demonstrate integrity, inspiring others to do the same.

Let's look at a practical example. Have you heard of John Kralik? He's a man who turned his life around by incorporating an incredibly simple action into his routine. It sounds like clickbait, but it is quite true. He was at a low point where everything seemed to be going wrong for him. He was being dragged down by a messy divorce, his relationships with his children were near estrangement, his small law firm was failing, his health wasn't the best, and his girlfriend had ended things with him. But he found ways to keep his chin up and move on with his life.

In 2011, Kralik published a book on his experiences, titled *A Simple Act of Gratitude*, detailing how he sent a handwritten thank-you note to one person a day for 365 days. When he changed focus from all that he was losing to everything he still had, Kralik found that offering gratitude without expecting anything in return bolstered the mood of people around him. Even though it did nothing directly for his ongoing struggles, it gave him strength.

All John Kralik did was be kinder to the people around him, but he still received the good that he put out into the world. It seems that the cosmos was kind to him in return: He turned his life around and found success in his subsequent endeavors. Would you call the positive changes in his life karma?

Karma teaches us that every choice we make, no matter how small, has an impact, and by living with intention and mindfulness, we can create positive outcomes for ourselves and others. We will talk more about this and the hope in modern-day practices in Chapter 6.

The Law of Cause and Effect

Earlier, I touched on the law of causality. It is the cause-and-effect process through which karma works to manifest itself across various lives. It can be quick, with results visible soon or in the same life. Or, based on your deeds from a long time ago, it can hit you in a future life.

Let me simplify this with the ever-popular analogy of planting seeds and harvesting the fruit of your labor.

Immediate and Delayed Outcomes

Say you have space in your yard for two large plants. The soil is fresh and nutrient rich. You sow a sunflower seed in one area and bury a bamboo shoot in the other. If you nurture both plants in the way they need, you influence them with your good deeds and intentions. Let's see what this brings you.

The sunflower seed sprouts in a matter of days, quickly growing a shoot and a root. Leaves unfurl and grow, and the stalk pushes up to the sunlight, blossoming into a large and brilliant sunflower with golden petals gleaming under the sun.

The bamboo shoot remains underneath the soil for a long time. Months pass by, and you might not see it. You continue to water and fertilize the soil, adding the right kind of compost as needed. Then, one day, you notice leaves peeking up from the earth. Several thin, hollow stalks push up through the ground. Suddenly, your yard is brimming with baby bamboo shoots, all of which grow around the same time.

Did you know that bamboo is classified as a type of grass? It spends long years growing roots under the soil before the shoots and leaves sprout for us to behold. But once it grows, it doesn't stop! In this example, it's similar to delayed karma.

Here's a breakdown of these two types of karma:

- **Immediate karma:** Your current karma, or *kriya-mana* karma, is the instantaneous consequences of your decisions and actions. You can face the repercussions or reap the rewards right after your choices have changed a situation.

- **Delayed karma:** This can come in two forms. It may be the accumulated outcomes, also called *sanchita* karma, which is comprised of the overall consequences of your actions from all your past lives that have yet to take effect. Delayed karma can also be *agami* karma. This is where your current actions have consequences by the end of your life or in your future lifetimes.

Remember that karma should not be valued just for its good or bad consequences. It is an external force demonstrating how our deeds naturally lead to certain results, some of which take time to manifest while others happen sooner than we expect.

Karma in Different Cultures

Buddhism

This religion emphasizes the intention behind the action. Rather than believing in the soul, it teaches that life is about what we can genuinely influence. In fact, Buddhists do not consider a soul to be an incorporeal "thing" that exists without the mind and the body. Instead, they consider it an expression of everything a person can be that exists between the stages of lives.

Rather than their verbal or physical exertion, a person's emotional state and purpose have more weight. I see this as an interesting take because we can lie through words and be disingenuous through actions, but our innermost thoughts and feelings are always true. For example, your friend may compliment you just so that you feel obliged to help them. But that act serves their self-interest; it's not rooted in kindness. So, in the Buddhist belief system, their karma is dependent on the intention as well and not just the compliment.

Buddhism relies on seven factors aside from the intention behind an action. In total, these are the right intention, view, speech, effort, action, livelihood, mindfulness, and concentration. By "right," I mean a well-balanced approach and not necessarily moral rightness. A believer would weigh the value of these eight aspects that can influence their karma.

When we look at Tibetan Buddhism, we learn that central to this sect is the concept of *bardos*. A bardo is a gap or an intermediary state between lives. According to the teachings, we experience three forms of death bardos. These are the states of dying, *dharmata*, and becoming.

- **Painful bardo of dying:** This is the transitional state that occurs at the moment of death. The consciousness senses the physical end and is in a state of confusion and pain.

- **Luminous bardo of dharmata:** Once the first bardo has been experienced, the dharmata follows. Here, the self experiences bright awareness and clarity of the gap between lives.

- **Karmic bardo of becoming:** This is the bardo following dharmata, where the self gets a sense of the consequences of its actions. It signifies the beginning of the next life and is where the consciousness finds a new body in which it will experience these repercussions.

Hinduism

This faith considers karma within the concept of *dharma*, which translates to "one's righteous duty." It is impersonal but ever present. There is more at play here when we look at the cosmic structure around our lives. Simply put, good actions lead to positive results, and bad actions lead to negative consequences. Whether karma is good or bad depends on your behavior or the duty you must undertake. It manifests in your future lives, influencing health, financial and social status, and other experiences you will face. The karmic cycle can be broken through attaining freedom, known as moksha, which is when the soul can break away from the reincarnation cycle.

Jainism

Here, karma is a moral force and is bound to the cycle of rebirth. It is similar to Hinduism in that karma indicates the consequences of actions. But people can work on it and seek liberation from the unending cycle to attain moksha. They can achieve this by living according to the religion's code of conduct, which involves self-discipline, meditation, and spiritual practice.

Sikhism

In this religion, the law of karma is about cause and effect. Similar to Jainism, karma secures the soul in the cycle of reincarnation. The cycle can affect the consciousness of all living beings, with humans considered the highest on the totem pole. The understanding is that making moral choices leads to positive karma, which can push you toward moksha. Immoral and hurtful choices can beget bad karma, which can drag you down and condemn you to be born as an animal in the next life.

Taoism

Here, karma is quite different from Hinduism and Buddhism. In Taoism, believers understand that the universe and life are built on a person's choices. Free will is a central idea of the Tao. Karma is the flowing energy that upholds the idea that our choices have a real impact on our lives and the world. Positive choices lean toward positive karma, which yields more power on the constructive and helpful end of the Taoist three-pole model, which is comprised of positive, neutral, and negative.

Having greater positive power gives you better odds of making good choices in life. Taoist principles see karma as a cosmic equilibrium where positive, negative, and even neutral deeds balance out everything in the end, so people can try to gain power despite making negative choices.

Native American

Nations

Indigenous tribes in North America have incredibly varied and fleshed-out ideas of the spiritual world. They also propose that the way to rise above the outcomes of thought and action is to stop acting for personal gain and genuinely make good choices.

- The Hopi believe in karma, stating that our actions in this life will have unavoidable consequences in future lives should we be reborn.

- The Oglala Lakota tribe sees the being Skan as the motion of the universe. The name translates to "to do, to act, to move about." Skan judges us based on actions and informs us that we cannot stop what is in motion and must let things play out.

Judaism

This religion has a concept called *Middah k'neged Middah,* which loosely translates to "measure for measure." In other words, what goes around tends to come around. You will find this explained in the Hebrew Bible in Isaiah 3:10–11, which says, "Hail the just man, for he shall fare well; He shall eat the fruit of his works. Woe to the wicked man, for he shall fare ill;

As his hands have dealt, so shall it be done to him" (Schechter, 2017).

While this is similar to the cosmic karma that prevails throughout multiple lives, it is not the same since, in Judaism, many consequences may be realized only on the Day of Judgment.

Christianity

Here, you will find the statement "a man reaps what he sows" from Galatians 6:7–8 (Biblia, n.d.). This is relevant to the Day of Judgment, where the fruit of the labor that a person has carried out all through their existence is realized only after death. Therefore, in Christianity, karma does not necessarily influence anyone during their life, as it does in many of the religions I've mentioned above.

But some orthodox Christians discuss the transmigration of souls, as seen in the Harvard Divinity School article "Flesh and Fire: Reincarnation and Universal Salvation in the Early Church" by Charles Stang, director of the Center for the Study of World Religions. The author is also a professor of early Christian thought. In the article, Dr. Stang speaks about Origen, an ascetic and early Christian scholar who was alive in the late 2nd and early 3rd century C.E. (2019):

> [Origen] believed the apostle Peter foretold of
> [God to be "all in all"] when he spoke in the

Acts of the Apostles 3:21 of a "restoration of all things" (*apokatastasis pantôn*). Origen took Peter at his word: *all* things, *all* the fallen minds, including Satan, must be restored—in other words, he insisted on universal salvation, but worked out across many lifetimes and successive worlds—in other words, reincarnation. ((Re)incarnation section)

Islam

This religion teaches of the Day of Judgment, where believers are to be judged after death for their deeds to determine their placement in heaven or hell. The All Mighty does not seek to offer rewards or punishments during life. Although the concept of karma is not mentioned in the Qu'ran or the Hadith, it is believed that the consequences of all actions will be seen only post-death.

New Age Spiritualism

This understanding views the law of karma as functioning in relation to a person's actions and thoughts. New Age Spiritualists adopted it from the ancient writings of Hinduism and Buddhism. The belief is that every act has consequences in this life and the next. Simply put, good decisions (powered by beneficial emotions of love, harmony, and the like) bring positive karma, and bad ones (such as hate and conflict) bring negative karma.

Karma Through Narrative

Various cultures have taught karma and its effects through several media, such as oral history, poetry, fantastical stories, or simply by living the ideal lifestyle that all people should.

The fables attributed to Aesop, who would have lived around 620 B.C.E., are long-lasting examples of this idea. His hundreds of short tales with clear morals are still relevant more than two millennia later! Narrated in a conversational tone, many of Aesop's stories feature anthropomorphized animals with a straightforward mentality whose words or choices lead to inevitable results. Perhaps the moralistic aspect does not connect to karma, but it shows how the storyteller lived to spread his message across the land and beyond time itself.

King Ashoka of India was another such role model. He was the third ruler of the Mauryan dynasty, which was in power between 300 B.C.E. and 200 B.C.E. He commanded a grand army and successfully amassed lands and kingdoms under his rule. But when he came across Buddhism and its tenets of karma, he let go of his military expansion and chose to rule through righteousness instead. This form of victory through truth won over the people of new lands, and Ashoka spread the teachings of Buddhism across regions, emphasizing its peaceful philosophies by becoming a just and effective monarch.

Perhaps you know people who are not particularly religious or spiritual yet stand by the idea of karma. One such believer was Charles Dickens. He touched upon the validity of consequences based on actions and even reincarnation in his semi-autobiographical novel, *David Copperfield* (1850). More to the point, Dickens's other notable works, including *The Pickwick Papers* (1837), *Oliver Twist* (1838), and even *A Christmas Carol* (1843), show grave instances of karma as retribution on characters whose choices have gone unchecked by society. It is mainstream narratives like these texts that have kept the philosophy alive in atheistic circles.

People before you have found wonderful wisdom and insight from believing in karmic traditions, and people long after you will do the same.

Modern Practices

Cultural and religious faiths like the ones we've just discussed are still practiced to an orthodox extent. Cases of belief in karma and living life based on its guidelines are also striking but not rare. For example, you may know people who tend to offer kindness to strangers if they themselves have had a good day. Rather than just attributing it to a selfish understanding, some may consider it along the lines of "what goes around, comes around."

A recent study conducted by Aiyana Willard and her team surveyed people of various religions to determine their behaviors in relation to the belief in karma and afterlife ideas. Published in Volume 41 of *Science Direct*, the paper, titled "Rewarding the Good and Punishing the Bad," states (2020):

> This research demonstrates that religious beliefs impact how we think about the consequences (reward and punishment) of our actions and how we think about moral norms. These findings suggest that it is not just being religious that matters but rather the content of one's beliefs. (General discussion section)

If you do good with the intention of simply being a good person rather than being perceived as one, your karmic results may differ. Despite my sounding like that fast-paced voice

at the end of a pharmaceutical commercial, I think you can
follow what I mean here.

Misconceptions About Karma

Let's get this cleared up. Simply put, karma is not fate. That's
kismet you're thinking of.

Karma is the force that determines how your intentions,
behaviors, and actions result in certain outcomes, either in
this life or the next. Sometimes, these outcomes happen way
down the line and are based on all your actions in previous
lives, as I mentioned above. It goes against the randomness
of luck as well. Karma is dependent on your intentions and
actions—this is the cause-and-effect connection according to
which it functions.

Your karma is created based on your free will. The future is in
your hands and not decided by a higher power.

Spector's Karma

I always found the story of Phil Spector to be one where
karma certainly played a role. Spector was a music producer
known for his innovative approaches, which elevated his career in Hollywood. In 2003, however, he was arrested for the
murder of actress Lana Clarkson.

What ensued was a dreadful set of circumstances where Spector's fame interfered with the process of court justice. The

trial dragged on for years before he was found guilty of second-degree murder and sentenced to prison in 2009.

Spector's conviction ended his career and freedom. Despite being an influential figure in the history of rock music, his reputation did not recover, and his personal life spiraled out of his control. During his imprisonment, Spector's health suffered, and he later developed tumors in his airway that took away his voice. He was shifted to a prison hospital, where he stayed for several years until he died from COVID-19 in 2021.

His imprisonment was due to his actions; however, the state of his health was coincidental. Some may call it karma, but that is not the truth.

Many liken karma to justice. I think this is an open-ended topic. Can we truly say that Lana Clarkson's family and friends felt that justice was served? Was Spector losing his high-profile career and success enough to soothe the agony of the brutal passing of a wonderful person? But it is clear that Phil Spector met the consequences of his actions, and it was no one's fault but his own, which is where karma does play a role.

Take this moment to pause and reflect on your developing beliefs about karma. Now that you know it has more to do with your choices and actions, how much power does it have over your life? How much control do you exercise over your days? Consider the moments when you've realized you're stuck with what you've done and have had to accept what's coming.

When you actively explore these ideas about your existence and the impact you make, karma can be an empowering force. It reminds you that you build your future brick by brick. Abrahamic faiths interpret this differently, stating that karma is enforced by a higher power or is part of the grand scheme of the universe. However, true karma, as elaborated by Buddhism and many other Eastern religions, is not an invisible force that decides when to reward or punish anyone.

Don't worry if you had the wrong idea about fate and karma before reading this book. We will cover these misconceptions and skepticism in more detail in Chapter 5.

Building Better Relationships

The impact of your past actions on current relationships is profound because you remember the things your friends and family have done for you and vice versa. As you build a mindful routine to invite good karma into your life, you will find its positive influence spreading to the people around you.

Say two best friends have shared many positive life experiences for decades. They have supported each other through adversity and built a strong relationship based on mutual respect. But should one friend betray the other, even unintentionally, it can create insecurity in themselves and their bond. If not addressed well, this past hurt can resurface and ruin the foundation of their relationship. On the other hand, if they do manage to communicate candidly about the pain and betrayal and apologize effectively, they can go on to rebuild the friendship. It may even be stronger than it was before.

Conflict Resolution Techniques

Take into account what you expect from karma and make choices that help and benefit your relationships. Let these exercises guide you moving forward:

Effective Communication

Open and honest communication makes any partnership strong. This is relevant for both personal and professional relationships. Listen clearly to the people you converse with, express your thoughts and feelings, and don't just offload them onto others. Consider the point of dialogue. Do you talk to make yourself louder or to convey ideas? What does the situation demand? Taking a step back to consider these factors reduces misunderstandings in relationships.

Active listening exercise: Set some time aside for this activity. Pair up with a partner and take turns expressing your perspective on a shared personal experience. During both turns, the listener must practice active listening by summarizing what the speaker said *before* responding. This helps improve your understanding of each other's points of view and builds empathy.

Informed Choices

Make decisions based on how they impact your relationships. Be thoughtful about your actions and find out as much as you can about a situation before you leap into problem-solving mode. Oftentimes, we stumble when we make split-second choices without a second thought. Take your time when possible. Avoid just giving orders to people or your team at work; instead, make plans or strategize with their input. This measured approach can change the way people perceive you, and they will value your choices more when you value theirs.

Role-playing scenario: You can find a partner to work with you on this or have several people join to make it a team-building activity. Create a scene that involves a conflict and role-play different responses. For example, you can present a work-related problem where a bottleneck threatens to hold up progress. Have everyone suggest an idea to resolve the issue. Each participant should discuss the potential outcomes of their choices. Encourage them to ask questions to learn more about the problem. It will help everyone reflect on how informed decisions can lead to better conflict resolution.

Proactive Responses

Avoid sudden reactions as much as you can. I don't mean you must not allow yourself to feel your emotions. Rather, when you employ mindfulness techniques every day, you learn to distance your emotions from your external responses, making it easier to be proactive and constructive in difficult situations.

Say you are facing a hurdle at work or home. As soon as you become aware of it, take the initiative to settle your temper. Consider all the facts and then brainstorm solutions. By doing so, you can pour your focus into the people around you rather than worry excessively about the problem. It also helps you refine your approach by ensuring the same problem does not crop up again. When possible, opting for prevention is more desirable than finding a cure because it shows your commitment to making things better at a foundational level.

Conflict anticipation worksheet: You may have met people who believe that anticipating problems will encourage them to happen. But this is not true. You are merely preparing. Sit as a group or on your own and focus on a challenge that affects your productivity or home life. Write down the hurdles you have seen connected to this scene. Identify common triggers or potential conflicts. Write down proactive strategies you can implement on your own or with someone's help to address these challenges before they arise. This encourages forward-thinking and preparedness.

This is the exceptional power of karma in our lives. By making the right choices, we can influence our fates and build a hopeful future for ourselves, whether in this life or the next.

Chapter 2

Reincarnation Explored

*When I discovered reincarnation, it was as if I
had found a universal plan I realized [...] that
there was a chance to work out my ideas. Time was
no longer limited. I was no longer a slave to the
hands of the clock.* –Henry Ford

Speaking of building a hopeful future, let's see what this
notable figure of history thought about the soul travers-
ing through various lives.

Henry Ford is known for many things, from pioneering in-
ventive cars to winning acclaim and awards for his work.
But did you know that he was a believer in the soul having
multiple lives? At the burgeoning age of 26, he came upon
the concept of reincarnation and understood how intrinsic
it could be to his world, where productivity meant so much.
Ford believed that work carries greater value when we can
carry our experience into the next life (Viereck & Ford, 1928).

In the previous chapter, I breezed through the concept of samsara. Let's cover it in detail here.

The Cycle of Birth and Rebirth

Samsara refers to the reincarnation cycle in which people are reborn into new lives based on their karma. Throughout this process, the soul remains more or less constant, only changing as it absorbs and learns from experiences. Our understanding is that the soul is our consciousness and that it makes up our personality, strengths, weaknesses, the thoughts and ideas we offer the world, and the actions we take that influence everyone around us.

Our soul is not a physical entity but a concept that builds our awareness. When a soul inhabits a body, there is life. At the point of death, the soul leaves the body and is later reborn into another one. The new life might not always recall memories and lessons learned from the previous incarnation, but some of us do remember. Some souls bring experiences and personality traits from their previous lives.

An Analogy of a Lifetime

I suppose you can relate this concept of rebirth to the process of progressing through successive grades in school. In this analogy, students are the souls, and grades are different lives. When the kids enroll in classes, they learn lessons and gain knowledge that they can use for the rest of their lives.

The students go through various grades as they advance, absorbing new experiences and evolving as they move on. They run into challenges and grow from failures, as does anyone. Beyond scoring wins and losses, they also learn the lessons of compassion and wisdom, which can be used in their next lives. At the end of every grade, their knowledge and skills are evaluated. If they pass, their positive karma increases, but if they fail, their negative karma increases.

In the school of samsara, no student can be held back. They must move to the next grade, but unlike a normal school, there is no senior year. How long it will take is not predetermined, yet the goal is to graduate from the school of life. This is moksha or liberation. You may have heard it being called "attaining nirvana." This happens once the student has learned all the necessary lessons from the curriculum to understand the nature of spiritual existence. Life is a continuous journey of learning, which we don't restrict to just one aspect. At every point on this voyage, there is something to discover and understand.

The Purpose of Reincarnation

While karma connects the actions of every life across a soul's journey, we can observe how the process of reincarnation builds the meaning of a soul. To call a person an "old soul" is to refer to their ideas, intentions, and actions as holding some kind of worldly wisdom that seemingly exceeds their age. You might have come across young children who are perceptive and precocious—more so than their peers. Perhaps they were nurtured that way, or perhaps nature took on a stronger role in influencing them.

While different philosophies interpret samsara in various ways, it generally encompasses the idea of impermanence and the importance of ethical living to break free from the cycle of rebirth. From this, we can say that reincarnation offers us several chances to better ourselves and find ways to attain nirvana. We can falter, stumble, make mistakes, fail at objectives, be rejected from opportunities, and still turn things around to win the grand game. If there are lessons that we are unable to learn in our first life, we can pick them up in our second. This is the line of thought that encourages us to keep going despite the seeming endlessness. It is only truly endless if we give up on trying to learn.

You must actively choose to develop empathy and understand different perspectives. Learn to overcome obstacles by being mindful of your abilities and surroundings. Refine your traits with every chance and life you get. It is a long journey, but it is the way the universe shows us that we are all deserving of another opportunity to find peace and liberation.

Historical Perspectives on Reincarnation

Cultures from the grand eras of the past have put their faith in this spiritual philosophy. I, for one, appreciate how civilizations across oceans have believed in such similar ideas of reincarnation, thanks in part to the spread of information. Ancient trade routes were impeccable and active, carrying goods, people, and bold new knowledge across the lands. Now, we can relax in our homes and learn about what our ancestors and neighbors thought of samsara.

Ancient India—The Upanishads

Upanishad is Sanskrit for "sitting nearby with devotion." The term refers to a large collection of ancient Vedic texts that cover the concepts of the soul's life cycle, as followed in Hinduism. They were penned from even older oral traditions of beliefs in reincarnation. The soul or spirit is the atman, which is eternal and cannot be destroyed. It is propelled through the cycle, influenced by karma and accumulating actions and consequences with every life.

The Upanishads promote these philosophies and emphasize the importance of self-awareness, inner nature, and true peace. These are the traits that the soul must learn and imbibe to break away from samsara and attain moksha.

Ancient Egypt—Psychostasia

Ancient Egyptian records talk about an afterlife where deceased souls are judged according to the goodness of their actions before achieving liberation or condemnation. The process of judgment is presided over by Osiris, the god of death and resurrection. It also involves the deity Ma'at, who is the overarching goddess of truth, justice, morality, order, harmony, and related themes.

In the judgment process, known as psychostasia, Osiris uses a set of balancing scales to judge the soul of the deceased by weighing their heart against a single fair feather of Ma'at's. If the heart is lighter, the soul will flourish in the paradisiacal

Field of Reeds. If it is heavier than the feather, the soul will be condemned to be devoured by the crocodile deity Ammit.

The ancient Egyptians also believed in resurrection, as Osiris had managed it with the help of his devoted wife, Isis. He was once resurrected into spirit form after his brother Set killed him to gain dominion over the kingdom.

And have you heard of the *Book of the Dead*? It is an ancient text that holds inscriptions and spells that priests could use to influence souls to reincarnate into new bodies and gain a second chance at finding favorable judgment. But this is only a small part of what the book really offers, and, thus, reincarnation is not observed as a grand belief of this culture. Rather, the Egyptians' focus was on the soul's journey through life and the afterlife, as opposed to its return to a new body.

As you will see, ancient Egyptians certainly influenced several other equally famous cultures.

Ancient Greece—Metempsychosis

The philosopher and mathematician Pythagoras was known for more than his mathematical theorems. He was a powerful orator and scholar, too. Additionally, he was a believer in reincarnation and lived his life under the idea that his actions would influence his karma. He referred to it as the transmigration of the soul (or metempsychosis). This is where a person's soul can travel through various bodies and be reincarnated based on their actions in previous lives. For this reason, Pythagoras remained a pious vegetarian, believing that all animals contained the soul of a past human.

His followers, Pythagoreans, also imbibed this teaching. Across ancient Greece, they propagated the idea that the soul could inhabit various forms of life. Nonbelievers prevailed as well, especially those who took great pleasure in hunting wildlife for the sake of spiting him and his followers.

Some have called Pythagoras the inventor of the concept of reincarnation in Western ideologies, but that's not true. He based a lot of his ideas on Egyptian texts, which were ancient even to his generation. This is what James Lutche has to say on the matter, as written in his paper, "Pythagoras and the Doctrine of Transmigration," published in 2008:

> Pythagoras is simply changing the path and the destination of the soul—it now has a capacity to move along through differing bodies, each being a microcosm of the All. Once the soul has seen the All, has been the All, as the story goes, it will be the All. (p. 5)

If you have gone through an ancient mythology phase at any point, you will instantly grasp the nuances of this idea across diverse cultures. It's a belief system that has been in place for thousands of years and interpreted differently by many people throughout various periods. In ancient societies, it marked the importance of living morally, as actions in this life determine our fate beyond death.

Modern Practices

You can also see the influence the cycle of rebirth has on modern-day religious ideas. For millennia, it has influenced the lives of millions of people across cultures, dynasties, and kingdoms scattered around the globe.

Meditation for Enlightenment

In Buddhism, the concept of rebirth is central to its teachings. Siddhartha Gautama, the Buddha himself, achieved enlightenment after years of dedicated meditation and following the rituals and philosophies of his religion. He achieved this circa the 6th to 4th century B.C.E., and those rituals have stood the test of time because Buddhists of today endeavor to accomplish what he did. Ceremonies such as Uposatha or Buddha pujas are conducted to pray for karma and consequences to be aligned positively. These rituals emphasize the connection between this life and future ones as well as the importance of learning and practicing compassion and ethical living.

Sacred Funeral Rites

In Hinduism, funeral rites are called *antyeshti*. They are deeply rooted in the belief in the cycle of birth, death, and rebirth. The rituals performed during a funeral help the soul transition to its next life. After the ceremony begins, the body is cremated, and the ashes are spread into a sacred river, essentially returning the physical construct to nature. Family members and priests often perform specific rites to ensure that the deceased's soul reaches an agreeable rebirth, reflecting that they look on the karma of previous lives favorably in the hope that this will help the soul experience good fortune in their next life.

Scientific Investigations

It's easy to look up qualified scholars who have spent years of their careers focused on uncovering the mysteries of reincarnation and past lives. These professionals have investigated old texts and gone into the field to find people with real past experiences who provide detailed and unerring accounts of experiences from previous lives. Beyond the below discussion, I encourage you to explore the research they've conducted in the interest of connecting unexplained modern scenarios with similar situations from eons ago.

Experts in the Field

Dr. Ian Stevenson

One of the most celebrated minds in the field was Dr. Ian Stevenson. As a leading psychiatrist and a professor at the University of Virginia School of Medicine, he founded the Division of Perceptual Studies. Dr. Stevenson was known for his detailed research and documentation on cases of children and adults who claimed to remember past lives. It's not for nothing that he was famous. He went in-depth to verify these claims and report that many of these children could explain scenes and memories from the past that turned out to be true, even when they had not been anywhere near the country or region they spoke of in their current lives. His work included numerous publications, such as *Twenty Cases Suggestive of Reincarnation* (1966), *Children Who Remember Previous Lives* (1987), and *European Cases of the Reincarnation Type* (2003).

Dr. Jim Tucker

Dr. Tucker, known for his keen eye for detail, has followed in Dr. Stevenson's footsteps to continue the work that continues to baffle and energize us. He is currently a psychiatrist at the University of Virginia and has undertaken more than two decades of work to research and learn from children with memories of past lives. His multiple publications have impressed the academic world, with works such as *Life Before Life: A Scientific Investigation of Children's Memories of Previous Lives* (2005) and *Return to Life: Extraordinary Cases of Children Who Remember Past Lives* (2013) having been translated into several languages for global distribution.

Dr. Carol Bowman

An author and researcher, Dr. Bowman is known for her work on children's past-life memories. She has gone on to work with people to uncover old memories through past-life regression therapy. Her findings have been published worldwide, with *Children's Past Lives* (1997) and *Return From Heaven* (2001) having gained momentum in the field of reincarnation research. Her works dive deep into cases of children who report memories of previous lives and discuss the implications of these experiences.

Dr. Erlendur Haraldsson

An Icelandic psychologist and parapsychiatrist, Dr. Haraldsson was known for his extensive research on reincarnation, apparitions, and psychic phenomena on similar themes. His work covered many cases of people, particularly in Sri Lanka and India, recalling memories from past lives. He has written several articles and books on these topics, with detailed research behind every case and his analysis of the overarching meaning of reincarnation. His most notable books, *At the Hour of Death: A New Look at Evidence for Life After Death*

(2012) and *I Saw a Light and Came Here: Children's Experiences of Reincarnation* (2017), have been bestsellers.

Research Methodologies

Experts with the appropriate education and training in the relevant fields are the best for this job. It is not easy work sifting through the lives of so many complex and layered individuals to find out whose memories are true.

For example, a researcher may conduct field studies in regions where beliefs in reincarnation are prevalent. This could involve observing cultural practices, engaging with local communities, and documenting firsthand accounts of reincarnation beliefs and experiences. It could also establish a foundation for their documentation that would differ from other types of work that look into the same regions.

Case Studies

Firsthand accounts of recalled past lives are rare but not impossible to track down. Researchers must go into the field to find valid case studies and examine if a subject's recollection of memories in conjunction with a past life is more or less correct. They cannot be completely objective about this because the experience happens within the mind and soul. It also helps to compare cases of reported reincarnation across different cultures and contexts to identify similarities and differences. This could involve examining cultural beliefs, societal attitudes, and historical contexts related to reincarnation.

Interviews

Gathering qualitative data is key to understanding real accounts of reincarnation. The researcher must record interviews, document memories, and compare the accounts with historical records to validate the claims as much as possible. They could post surveys based on the relevant culture, religion, and region for people to take, allowing them to gather broad data on beliefs and experiences similar to reincarnation. They might also create charts to show a skeleton structure of what their team should be on the lookout for.

Health Assessments

There's a reason Dr. Ian Stevenson built a successful career with his studies and research into children's recollections of past lives. His background in psychiatry helped him understand the mental health and cognitive functioning of people from various walks of life, and his understanding helped his team rule out psychological explanations for the patients' experiences of unexplained memories and sensations.

Regression Therapy

Some researchers use reposeful hypnosis or guided past-life regression techniques to help individuals access memories of previous lives. This method can help them recall experiences that may not be readily available in their conscious memory. The results are then analyzed for patterns or common themes. However, this therapy must be conducted by a qualified expert who understands the person's psychological state and has a desire to find out the truth.

Difficulty of Proof

Researchers have also faced significant difficulties in proving reincarnation scientifically. The entire area is inherently subjective. We're talking about personal experiences and memories that nobody else but the person in question can bear witness to. Skeptics will therefore question why they should believe that others have experienced such unexplained parapsychological phenomena when they themselves haven't. Distinguishing genuine memories from figments of a vivid imagination, religious beliefs, or psychological conditions is also necessary work for psychiatrists and other experts to undertake.

We know without a doubt that dreams happen. But that's because nearly everyone on the planet recalls their dreams. Even animals dream vividly enough to start pawing and hissing in their sleep. Memories of past lives are so much rarer and simply cannot be verified in a standardized way. Most people lack concrete historical documentation or objective evidence. The most common and obvious signs have been people speaking another language they never learned or even heard. Sometimes, children recall specific conversations that families or friends of the deceased can verify. But the instances that have been proved are the outliers.

Interdisciplinary Approaches

Different fields contribute to understanding reincarnation by tackling the layered and shrouded vagueness around every case. I believe that psychology, anthropology, religious studies, history, and even neuroscience can provide answers to different components of the major question. For example, psychology examines the cognitive and emotional aspects, while anthropology offers a cultural context on how belief in reincarnation influences society in general.

The whole is certainly greater than the sum of the parts in this case. We must consider the subjective experiences of individuals and the broader cultural and historical narratives that inform those experiences, and it takes a village to get these answers, as you will see in the many case studies I will discuss in the next chapter. By combining insights from all the mentioned disciplines, researchers can develop a better understanding of reincarnation.

Chapter 3

Real-Life Tales of Reincarnation

We all have some experience of a feeling, that comes over us occasionally, of what we are saying and doing having been said and done before, in a remote time—of our having been surrounded, dim ages ago, by the same faces, objects, and circumstances. –Charles Dickens

Experts who study reincarnation and past-life concepts tend to focus on case studies that involve more substantial detail. A child who reports memories that an adult cannot explain away has a better chance of falling into this category than one who reports odd sensations at peculiar hours. The better the description, the better the chance of acceptance.

Meticulous record-keeping and verification of claims contribute to a refined field. Reincarnation studies typically examine the stories of people who claim to have lived before, exploring their accounts of past-life memories and tracing recognizable names and places. Researchers conduct detailed interviews with them, their families, and even individuals connected to their past lives to corroborate the information as much as possible.

Children Remembering Past Lives

Leininger and Huston

James Madison Leininger's story is arguably one of the most famous cases out there. He was born in 1998 to Bruce and Andrea Leininger. As a toddler, he exhibited an unusual interest in airplanes, to the point of having nightmares of plane crashes. When he grew into a young child and became able to articulate his odd sensations, Leininger spoke about flying a plane as a pilot during World War II.

His details were oddly specific. He could name the parts of a fighter plane, stating that he'd flown as a fighter pilot in his past life. His parents were unsure of what to make of his claims, but the people around him recognized that the historical details the child had given rang true. He turned out to recall specific instances of an adult man who had flown a Corsair plane during the war. James had also given the name of the boat—*Natoma*—the plane had supposedly taken off from. His nightmares showed him how he had been shot down by the Japanese forces in 1945.

Bruce Leininger began looking into the names and events his son spoke of and, after searching online, came across the U.S .S. *Natoma Bay*, an aircraft carrier ship that was in the Pacific during the war. He found a close match to a person who'd suffered the fate that James had dreamed of, a man named James Huston Jr. This was confirmed when he contacted Huston's sister, who had photographic proof that Huston Jr. had flown a Corsair.

James's mother, Andrea, contacted Dr. Carol Bowman, who helped guide the child through careful regression therapy to reduce the nightmares and negativity lingering from James's experiences.

The case was detailed in the book *Soul Survivor: The Reincarnation of a World War II Fighter Pilot*, published in 2009, which was featured on the *New York Times* Best Sellers list. Authors Bruce Leininger, Andrea Leininger, and Ken Gross emphasized how James was at the right age to recall the memories without too much subconscious tampering. Carol Bowman mentioned this in an ABC taping that focused on various case studies of reincarnation stories, "[Young kids] haven't had the cultural conditioning, the layering over, of experience in this life so that the memories can percolate up more easily. These memories tend to fade between the ages of five to seven" (Bowman, 2004, 4:38).

Dr. Jim Tucker was impressed by the strength and veracity of James's memory recollection and how it was proven with some thorough research. He managed to interview the

Leiningers in 2010 and compile a list of verified facts from James's memories, which were contributors to the validity of his case.

It is stories such as James's that give us hope for second chances at life. Many of us do not remember our past lives, but the knowledge that we might have had them can provide a softer landing to reality.

Common Themes

As you read more cases of purported and verified reincarnation, take note of the similarities with James Leininger's experience. Most cases share certain aspects. They include detailed memories of past lives, such as specific names, locations, and events. From what I've read, these accounts frequently involve a sense of familiarity with places or people the children have never encountered in their current lives.

It's no coincidence that these cases feature children who have clear recollections. You'll see that kids may express emotions or preferences that seem to align with their purported past experiences, such as a strong affinity for certain cultures or historical periods. These accounts can evoke a sense of wonder and curiosity about the nature of existence and the continuity of the soul. However, some stories also feature traumatic events from past lives, which can influence the child's behavior or fears in their current life. If reading their stories either gives you goosebumps or makes you raise your defenses, consider that, for the subjects, it is simply a reality. These strange and often painful memories are normal for them, and what they need is help overcoming the fear and stigma of speaking out loud.

Implications

The cases of children recalling past lives make us stop and think. Can consciousness continue through physical death? The reincarnation school of thought seems to believe this. So, if memory is not confined to a single physical existence, what else are we capable of?

I don't mean to imply that we must discard all forms of fear and embrace reincarnation without a second thought. Belief should be careful, guided, and beautiful. I do not use this word lightly. But why do we believe in something? When we throw all our effort and energy into working toward an idea, it means a great deal. Belief comes with a great sense of power and control. When used right, belief can open doors and build bridges of awesome potential.

That's why instances of reincarnation that seem so real help us raise intriguing questions about the nature of consciousness. These stories potentially indicate that the soul and mind can transcend physical death and persist in some form beyond the life of the body. Now, these recollections do not give definitive proof of consciousness surviving death, but they certainly broaden the discussion.

The Boy Who Lived Before

Macauley and Robertson

Cameron Macauley is another excellent candidate for our
humble research. This case reminds me of Shanti Devi's experiences (which we touched on earlier and will revisit later
in this chapter) because Cameron was just as strong-willed as
her, insisting that the memories of his past life were crucial.
He was born in 2000, near Glasgow. He expressed unusual

thoughts and memories about a boy from the Robertson family of Barra, an island off the coast of Scotland.

Cameron told his parents and older brother all about his other family in Barra, which comprised his mother, father, six siblings, a black dog with a white stripe, and an orange cat. They lived in a white house with a black dial phone and three toilets. Ever since he was two years old, the child mentioned his Barra family almost daily. By the time he started nursery school, he would wail for his Barra mother and pleaded almost every day to return to the island. News of his strange memories eventually became widespread.

Details Corroborated

Dr. Jim Tucker interviewed Cameron and the Macauleys and then flew with them to Barra to look up the Robertsons. However, it took a while for the research team to find a family who fit the description from Cameron's story. Eventually, they narrowed it down to a family who had vacationed on the island sometime in the 1960s and 1970s. The team tracked down one of the surviving sisters, Gillian Robertson, who confirmed that they'd had a black dog with a white patch at the time but did not have answers regarding her father being struck by a car—a significant detail Cameron remembered—or if her brother had passed away while on the island.

Cameron, unlike many children, was not hesitant to share details of his past life. It might be because the death he recalled seemed smooth and quick, contrary to other cases. Many children remember the dreadful details of their deaths and can even recall the pain and fear. Cameron, on the other hand, stated that he had fallen into a dark hole and then found his current mother, Norma Macauley. I think this seemingly smooth transition helped him cope with the reality of re-membering everything.

Thanks to his open nature and his willingness to answer Dr. Tucker's research team's questions, Cameron supplied them with ample evidence about the Robertson family, which they verified with enough validity to stun many people. Dr. Tuck-er included his notes on the case in the 2013 book *Return to Life: Extraordinary Cases of Children Who Remember Past Lives*.

Response and Acceptance

As Cameron's story gained attention, the Macauley fami-ly faced additional pressures from outside sources, includ-ing the media. This attention brought both supporters and naysayers, which threw a wrench in their regular lives. His parents and older brother, Martin, took his side when the me-dia hounds came knocking. Norma Macauley even countered the argument that Cameron might have absorbed fanciful ideas of a Barra family from something he'd seen on TV. She defiantly said that Cameron and Martin had been raised together and thus exposed to the same educational and en-tertainment material. Martin had no tales to tell of a different life or family, while Cameron had stated several facts about the Robertsons and had stuck to his words for over three years without pause.

When the Macauleys did find the opportunity to visit Barra and the house in question, Cameron plaintively admitted that he missed his Barra mother. The house had seemed to almost scare him because of how much things had changed over nearly four decades. But he returned home to Glasgow a calmer child, having found closure to the dull, throbbing aches of a life gone past.

Consciousness and Memory

The conscious mind is most concerned with the present moment in time. Certain events are embedded into the deepest layers of consciousness, while others flit away into short-term memory storage. The real struggle is remembering any memory as fully as possible.

Recalling an event is not an objective effort. Humans tend to misremember slight details, no matter how focused we are. Unless you have an eidetic memory of events where every detail is seared into your mind, be prepared to accept that your memory might differ from the experience it's based on.

This could happen to the extent that you may "remember" things that never happened. Such false memories are a bane but more common than you might think. For example, a child might swear they finished a chore in the morning only to realize later that they never even started it. Perhaps they conflated the vision of it with a past memory of a different day when they did complete the chore. False memories can be inferred or implanted in you. You need look no further than the 2010 movie *Inception*, which, if you understand that plot, is all about seeding a fake idea into the mind of the heir to a business empire.

This is what professional researchers must weed out when interviewing people who report memories that have no place in their current lives. Done properly, we end up with a pool of candidates whose memories likely correspond to a real person who had lived in the past. It is often a small pool, though vast and diverse if you know where to look.

Before we continue our discussion of famous case studies, let's take a look at how we can improve true memory recollection through guided hypnosis at the hands of a professional.

My Memories of a Past Life

I mentioned above how memory recollection is never perfect and how our own minds can fail us when it comes to recalling specific instances of life (any life). I had this problem. I went through life not knowing why I seemed to face such sorrow and hardship in my relationships. It would be one thing to understand why my behavior seemed to be at odds with fate itself, but I had no knowledge or memory to explain why my personality and attitude seemed to be tuned toward destructive tendencies.

This made it difficult to address my problems. I understood that simply fixing the symptoms did not do anything for the underlying cause. I had to dig deep. I had to approach this from a different angle.

Enter past-life regression (PLR) hypnosis and therapy. I brought memories of my past lives to the conscious level and interpreted them with the help of professional guidance. As a result, my PLR therapy sessions have offered me solace and hope for my future.

Past-Life Regression Sessions

I had been facing quite a lot of struggles when I finally chose to try hypnosis. I figured any help was good help. I found a qualified hypnosis therapist who had achieved great success with many clients, and I was eager to be the next. First, we sat down and hashed things out. I knew that proper recollection might only happen after a few sessions, so I was prepared to wait and follow through with all the appointments and hypnotic therapy sessions.

I found my groove. During deep sessions, I experienced a trance-like vision where I was less than real. Sometimes, I saw terrible visions featuring the dead body of a man who had hurt me in a previous life. Although this was difficult, it helped me realize that I'd had destructive relationships in the past, and the negativity had transferred over to my current life. I learned how to slowly let the memories play out and acknowledge that these events were in the past and that I need not hold on to them anymore. I had to make the conscious choice to let go of the pain and fear, even if it made me vulnerable for a time.

The dissonant relationship with my current mother was also rooted in a previous life. I remember being at odds with the adoptive mother from my past and discovered that I'd been adopted from a trying orphanage and taken into a home with similar disruptive circumstances. I also learned that my adoptive parents from back then had been reborn into my birth parents now.

Different people respond to PLR in various ways, but regression does not mean that you will sink into the memories. It shows you how to let them wash over you. A well-experienced therapist can guide you to appreciate the effort to move on from certain traumatic or inexplicable moments. Once you accept the past, you can let it go and come back to the present. Then, you can hope for a better future by preparing for it.

Realizations

There was a time when I felt stuck in a rut, forced to experience the same negative cycle of emotions and experiences with my mother and the men in my life. Now, everything is different. I have been able to find some answers to my situation and understand the destructive qualities of my thoughts and actions.

It is for the better that I have been able to reconcile the differences and find newer, more helpful ways to move on from the things I cannot change. PLR has shown me that the unhealthy relationships I had unwittingly been forming were a result of terrible incidents from a past life. I could not resolve the broken heart of my current body without understanding the truth behind the pain from that previous life.

From a personal standpoint, PLR has thrown open locked doors and thrust me into a brand-new direction. My journey through PLR therapy has also led me to reflect on the broader themes of existence, the nature of consciousness, and the concept of reincarnation. These ideas have been helpful to my recovery. This is why I wish to write and publish about my experiences. Having once been in a place with no answers in sight, I have no doubt that my therapy sessions have done me some serious good. I wish to pass on this good to you. If a single reader finds consolation in my words, I know I have helped *somebody* in the world.

More Modern Tales of Reincarnation

The Pollock Sisters

I love the fact that we have mixed responses to the concept of reincarnation. It shows that we can have varying ideas while still remaining in harmony with each other. As I have noted before, believing in something is no easy task. We cannot make someone believe in an ideal unless they understand its impact and genuinely wish to put their faith in it.

This next case is one that has fascinated me to no end. The Pollocks were a family in Britain, and the father, John, was a devout believer in reincarnation, while his wife, Florence, was not. It was a house of diverse beliefs, yet everyone supported each other as much as they could. The couple had four kids together and ran a busy grocery store in the 1950s. Their younger daughters, Joanna and Jacqueline, were inseparable. However, tragedy struck the family when the sisters were killed in a car accident.

John and Florence were devastated and had their own ways of coping with the devastation. But a while later, Florence was pregnant again and gave birth to twin girls, Gillian and Jennifer. Despite never knowing their older sisters, they seemed to recall quiet and even gory details of the deadly crash that nobody in the family had told them. In addition, Jennifer had two birthmarks on her body that were reminiscent of

Jacqueline's old birthmark and one of her scars. Gillian had obstinate personality traits that eerily resembled Joanna's.

John was convinced that his new twin daughters were reincarnations of the older girls they had lost. There were too many similarities to ignore, even though they were from the same family.

Confirmations Against the Skeptical

The first thought you might have after reading about the Pollocks is that the evidence might be against John's favor. Since Gillian and Jennifer were related to Joanna and Jacqueline, any similarity can be explained away by stating that "genetics" were responsible.

Yet, Dr. Ian Stevenson took great interest in the case. He flew over to Britain and interviewed the family over several sessions, helping them cope with the unexplained scenarios and also documenting the girls' memories, birthmarks, and experiences. Dr. Stevenson had researched more than 40 pairs of twin reincarnation cases throughout his career, of which the strongest study was the Pollock sisters. In 1997, he published *Reincarnation and Biology: A Contribution to the Etiology of Birthmarks and Birth Defects, Volume 2*, detailing this case.

This example shows that documenting these personal accounts does not just help keep track of everything that's said. It also shows how subjective notes can be put through the rigor to produce strong, verifiable evidence of true reincarnation. Qualified teams do not take memory recollection at face value. They focus on specific details that can be verified, such as names, locations, and events, with researchers like Dr. Ian Stevenson conducting extensive investigations into these cases and analyzing patterns and commonalities. Additionally, therapists also use PLR sessions to explore these claims and help the kids find peace with the unfinished business of their previous lives.

Those of us who believe are not looking to fool or hurt anyone, but there will always be criticism of these claims due to a lack of scientific data. I choose to take this as a positive thing. It keeps us on our toes and motivates us to find as much evidence as possible to help build a concrete case. But I do agree: It would be better to have unquestionable proof in the face of the unknown. When it comes to having these unbelievable experiences, it can be hard to find support and community. This is what researchers such as Dr. Stevenson, Dr. Bowman, Dr. Tucker, and more aim to do. They try to provide support from an authority's perspective. It means so much more than they can imagine.

A Western Understanding

It is far too simplistic to divide the world into East and West. While it does help us get the point across, I believe we should specify such details as far as we can to help us figure out exactly how to approach a concept. When we talk of reincarnation, past lives, and karma, the majority of us might associate it with Eastern traditions. Of course, this means Asia, the Arab world, and the Mediterranean. But Australia and Russia are also geographically located in the eastern hemisphere. Do we count them?

Most Caucasian settlements are considered part of the Western population. But people of Caucasian descent do have native origins and traditions, as you will find in Russia, the Czech Republic and Slovakia, Ireland, Scotland, and Wales, among others. Any time you hear of the East and West divide, be cognizant of the diverse people who may inhabit the space between.

Allow me to specify, then, what I mean by Western concepts when I talk of reincarnation and its philosophy in this book. By Western ideals, I mean the thoughts and philosophies of people in metropolitan regions of North America, Western Europe, and Australia. These communities generally approach the concept of reincarnation with a mix of skepticism and curiosity.

Urban communities in these regions favor evidence-based knowledge, science, technology, and progress. Alternatives are typically dismissed or, at best, tolerated—unless people actively choose to keep an open mind. However, being open to multiple views is not the preferred tradition of many religions. But, if we make an effort to read up on different traditions and interact with people of various religions, we start to connect ideas and find patterns across faiths. We can build spiritual open-mindedness regarding the validity of other-worldly instances, case in point: karma and reincarnation.

Reactions to reincarnation claims can vary widely, from out-right rejection to open-minded exploration. I will admit that these countries have a growing interest in spiritual and meta-physical topics, prompting some to explore reincarnation as a potential explanation for phenomena like déjà vu or un-explained memories. This duality reflects a broader cultural tension between actual evidence and helpful beliefs.

Some people may engage with the idea through literature, media, and personal anecdotes, often seeking to understand it in the context of reported personal experiences or phenom-ena. Others may participate in groups or practices that focus on PLR, viewing it as a therapeutic tool. Overall, the per-ception of reincarnation in Western societies is complex (as it is in Eastern regions) and influenced by individual beliefs, cultural background, and the interplay between science and spirituality.

Reincarnation Stories From Around the World

Shanti and Lugdi Devi

This famous case from India, which I briefly outlined earlier in the book, is one of the many that attracted teams of re-searchers to explore cultures where belief in reincarnation is more prevalent in the community. Lugdi Devi was a woman from Mathura who passed away a week after giving birth to her youngest son in 1925, leaving behind a grieving family.

Barely a year later, Shanti Devi was born just outside Delhi. As a four-year-old, she began speaking of another life where she was married with children. Shanti provided her parents with details about her past life as Lugdi, offering the names of her husband and children. She also recalled that she'd died after suffering from complications while giving birth. Despite their community's more favorable leaning toward the ideas of karma and reincarnation, Shanti's parents did not believe her claims at first. But when the descriptions grew more detailed and passionate, they investigated the names Shanti gave them.

The family traveled to Mathura, where Shanti recognized the environment enough to lead them straight to Lugdi Devi's house. She identified Lugdi's family members, including her bereaved husband, despite never having met them before.

You and I are not the only ones astonished by the story. The case attracted Dr. Ian Stevenson's attention. He conducted extensive interviews with Shanti and her family as well as Lugdi Devi's relatives. Dr. Stevenson documented his findings in his 1966 book *Twenty Cases Suggestive of Reincarnation*, where he presented Shanti Devi's case as one of the most compelling examples of past-life memories.

Uduji and Iregbu

Ngozi Uduji and her family were part of the Igbo tribe in
Nigeria, and they were believers in rebirth and past lives.
Ngozi was born sometime around 1970 without her left upper arm. She also had dark patches on her skin as a newborn,
although they faded within days. By the time she was two
years old, she'd admitted to her grandfather that she was the
reincarnation of Ogbonna Iregbu, her father's cousin who
had been killed in 1968 after he was caught in a market bomb-
ing during the Nigerian Civil War. The family had found his
body in the aftermath, with his left forearm almost discon-
nected from the limb. He'd also been covered in terrible burn
marks all over.

The tribe's diviner, too, had proclaimed Ngozi to be reincarnated from her Uncle Ogbonna. Ngozi was able to identify
Ogbonna's gardening tools from a shed that had not been
touched in years. As a toddler, she demonstrated the correct
usage of many of the tools to her grandfather. She was also
inclined to express herself with a boyish personality and preferred the company of boys until she grew older.

Ngozi Uduji's story was one of 57 instances that Dr. Ian
Stevenson documented when he was researching Igbo cases. He gave careful attention to memories where names and
events were recollected and where scars, injuries, or birthmarks on the subjects' bodies corresponded to something
their previous incarnation had experienced. He noted how

many communities scattered across the continent of Africa believed in reincarnation and even had tribal elders, healers, or diviners who'd been present for the child's birth and sensed they were in a reincarnated body.

Children who were born with atypical bodies, such as Ngozi with her missing forearm, were considered culturally important to their tribes. This tradition dates back to several thousand years ago when physical imperfections or disfigurements were thought to indicate a connection to higher spiritual or paranormal powers.

Wangdu and Rinpoche III

In 1987, Dezhung Rinpoche III, then a Tibetan Lama, said that Seattle would be his next birthplace. He was right. In 1989, Sonam Wangdu was born in the city and came to realize that he was the Tibetan Lama's fourth incarnation. His parents had even dreamed about the Lama in the months leading up to his birth. Now that's commitment!

Reincarnation is not seen as the most important aspect of the Tibetan Buddhist faith. It is just part of the soul's journey to freedom from the constant cycle of rebirth. As a soul learns more from every life, gaining more positive karma with each cycle, it grows closer to attaining liberation. The soul comes to know more about the universe and the karmic laws that govern us.

Reincarnation and Healing: Emotional Transformations

Reincarnation brings the possibility of healing and catharsis. We see this possibility with the Tibetan Buddhist understanding of it. Sonam Wangdu was one of the rare Lamas—out of hundreds—who "chose" to have their rebirth in the West. We rarely have a choice when it comes to such fates, but perhaps we can will it to happen as we grow closer to the end of the cycle. I, for one, am incredibly curious about it. I cannot say where I am in my journey, but my focus is to live to the fullest and gain as much as I can from my experiences. This is how I better my karma and nurture hope for a promising future.

Emotional Healing

Now, this is an understanding that has worked for me: Actions in our past lives can lead to certain consequences in our present day. Knowing this, the situations that have cropped up without obvious explanation now make more sense when we remember what has led to them. Life feels incredibly unfair when things hurt us, especially when we haven't done anything (to our knowledge) to deserve it.

Realizing the truth of our actions and feeling genuine remorse for unjust deeds are the real lessons we must take away from our soul's journey. This is only possible if we remember what we have chosen and the things we have done.

Professional and Guided Healing

When it comes to professional guidance and emotional healing, few do it better than Dina Kleiman. She has experienced her own catharsis when responding to life's bitter experiences and now reaches out to help others find their home.

As she says in this Medium article, "When we heal ourselves, we contribute to the healing of the world. By cultivating positive energy and compassionate actions, we can create ripples of healing that extend far beyond ourselves" (Kleiman, 2024, para. 4).

Kleiman has guided several patients through careful PLR sessions, helping them remember the "why" behind actions and consequences. Let's look at one of her success stories, Julie, who approached her to find energy and love in herself and help her develop a real care for her bodybuilding career.

Kleiman helped Julie find herself in a past life, where her soul was revealed to be a beautiful woman named Alvara. The woman even corrected Kleiman's pronunciation of her name and asked her to convey to Julie that this wonderfully strong and lovely warrior was her.

Julie managed to tune into this vision of the woman and found worth within herself. She learned that her soul had always been powerful, and she managed to find that power in this life as well. She has now turned her work into a dedicated vocation, guiding people to heal by helping them focus on their body's needs and health.

With every client Dina Kleiman helps, that person goes on to help others, causing a ripple effect of strength and kindness throughout the world.

This example shows that we are not just interconnected between lives; we touch each other and motivate people just by seeing the goodness in them.

Steps to Approach Past-Life Regression Therapy

1. Identify exactly what you wish to search and find. Do you want to address a certain phobia or fear? Do you have unresolved trauma from your childhood? How much are you willing to share with someone who, despite all their professional expertise, is a stranger to you? Write down what you want to address and the type of revelation you expect.

2. Find trained practitioners who understand and have experience in PLR therapy. Search online forums for client testimonials and reviews. Verify the therapist's qualifications and find trusted sources; from there, you can narrow down the list of potential practitioners.

3. Decide where you want to hold the sessions. The therapist may work with you in your home to offer

you a secure space or in a quiet office to give you a comfortable distance from your personal life. It might even help to bring a trusted friend who can sit with you and ensure you haven't missed any details.

4. Before any session, discuss your concerns and ideas with the therapist. Be as open as you can.

5. Keep an open mind when you talk to the therapist or start the session. Many a time, people have hang-ups or are skeptical about the approach, but the session is your choice. It is a serious endeavor and not a fun side activity. It can be interesting and enjoyable, or it can reveal sinister truths.

Preparation is most of the game. But I must caution you not to try this type of therapy on your own or without a qualified therapist. The simplest ways to go wrong involve mistaking a dream or fantasy for something that is real. But sinking into your subconscious is powerful and can often uncover things about you. A certified professional will help you cope with the truth and bring you back to the present.

However, you can certainly try the following techniques on your own!

- **Journaling:** This is a great activity that can work before, in between, or after your sessions. It helps you keep track of the ideas or thoughts you have or the memories and sensations you perceive. Writing your perspective also solidifies what you have experienced and makes it all the more real.

- **Breathing and exercise:** Perform mindful breathing and exercise routines and stick to them. These conscious body movements help your spatial awareness and help you understand the state of your body every day. They also contribute to your health and boost your emotional state.

- **Open discussions:** Talk to a trusted friend or relative about your experiences. Let them know how your sessions are going and keep a positive spin on things. Allow them to support you and lift your spirits. Avoid people who are skeptical about the approach. It takes a great deal of energy to defend your choices, especially when these decisions actively help you.

In this manner, you can use your past lives to work on your current situations, address problems, and find solutions. Do not ignore or reject the past. Learn from it and build a better, hopeful future for yourself. This is how you can connect the power of remembering your past lives with changing your karma. We will see more of that in the next chapter!

Chapter 4

The Intersection of Karma and Reincarnation

The physical world gives each one of us myriad opportunities to learn ultimately how to live in balance—harmony. The karmic strokes that seem harsh often turn out to be the best things that could happen. –Mary T. Browne

As I mentioned in the Introduction, remembering vital past moments that impact our present is a matter of luck, focus, and fate. You can seek out a professional hypnosis therapist to lead you through PLR sessions, though I advise you to try this out after much deliberation and consultation with experts. These sessions can increase your chances of remembering the truth of the past. For many, knowing this truth is helpful for understanding why they have experienced such mysterious upheaval. It shows that the cosmos is in balance and that there is meaning in why certain things happen.

Interconnected Journeys: Karma and Reincarnation

As we know, the nature of new lives is heavily influenced by the karma accumulated in past lives. Good karma may lead to a more favorable rebirth, while negative karma can result in challenges or hardships in future existences. Simply put, karma and reincarnation are intertwined to the extent that only when we understand how they function together can we use them to our advantage.

Karmic Debt

Your karmic debt refers to the consequences of actions that have accumulated over your many lives. What you incur will influence the future, as you well know by now. We must therefore consider the moral quality of this debt. It is generally equated with the negative karma a soul has racked up due to past thoughtlessness or poor choices.

The reincarnation cycle ensures that you get opportunities to erase the debt and build up positive karma. Everyone gets the chance they deserve to rectify their cosmic scorecard. This accumulation of your karma becomes your compass, showing you the better choices you must make to balance out your past actions. In a sense, while you allow fate to guide your actions, it is a fate you have constructed yourself.

Thus, we are encouraged to live ethically and mindfully, as every action has the potential to shape not only our current life but also our future incarnations. This is what most religions teach us. When we live decent lives, we will be judged accordingly. Karma and reincarnation show how living with goodness can benefit us across lives (if not within the same one). This interconnected relationship brings our eye to the importance of personal growth and transformation. You can tell a child to be good, but the child will learn this lesson best when they experience what being good can do for others and themselves.

Perhaps I seem philosophical here, but I speak from experience. Be aware of your strength and worth. Listen to the way your actions influence everything around you. Understand that you are a small but significant cog in the grand scheme of things. You are a minute speck in space, yes, but not ignorable. When you grow mindful of your actions, the consequences reflect change and improvement, leading your soul toward a better and more fulfilling life.

Incomplete Karma, Now Resolved

Dr. Carol Bowman's 2001 book, *Return From Heaven: Beloved Relatives Reincarnated Within Your Family*, makes for inspiring reading. It gives evidence-based accounts of young children with the same defining characteristics as their deceased relatives who passed away before the kids were born. When you get the chance to peruse this book, you'll see how every seeming coincidence makes up a grander picture that shows that we just might have another clue indicating that reincarnation is true.

Dr. Bowman writes of a young boy named Dylan, whose family believes he might be a reincarnation of his father's grandfather, Pop-Pop. Several odd behaviors that young Dylan exhibited were reminiscent of what Pop-Pop a retired beat cop turned prison guard, used to do. The old man was an avid street craps player and had smoker's lungs. He was restless and stubborn to the end, and he insisted on keeping his licensed gun under his pillow every night.

One day, Pop-Pop moved the gun without warning anyone. Given his ailing age, this was concerning. Dylan's dad, Mike, got rid of the loaded gun, which infuriated his grandfather, who never got over this betrayal and the loss of his weapon. Added to this, Pop-Pop had originally lived in a house that was located in a neighborhood where estate prices were falling. To safeguard their investment, Mike elected to sell the house and helped move Pop-Pop to a nicer duplex. The old man perceived this as being kicked out of his home and never forgave Mike for it.

After Pop-Pop's death, the family noticed that Dylan would always keep a toy gun on him, unwilling to be parted with it during his waking hours. The child pretended to smoke a lot, which couldn't be explained away since he was only two and had seen nothing but cartoons. At the time, no one in the family smoked, so his mother, Anne, couldn't understand where he might have copied the act from. This, coupled with a few other attitudes, could not be dismissed.

Mike and Anne admit that with Dylan's arrival, it was like Pop-Pop had moved back in with the family and had a good life now, one where he was allowed to keep his gun, smoke, play craps, and stay in the house he wanted to. These incidents show how karma may remain unaddressed in one life but can become fulfilled in the next.

Rebirth Resolution

This is but one of many examples where we can see that reincarnation gives a soul a real chance to find the resolution it was seeking. In this way, the more rebirths a soul experiences, the greater their odds are for real karmic resolution. They experience unfettered spiritual growth that allows them to learn from their various life experiences across the eons and build a strong positive karma balance. I've always found this uplifting. Each of the soul's lifetimes offers challenges and lessons, especially based on what we have done in the past. It is unique to the soul and helps it gain insights that normally would not be possible within only one lifetime.

With every incarnation, we can evolve spiritually and find greater understanding within ourselves and the world around us. This is how we can truly imbibe the worth of active decision-making skills. Plainly said, it is important to consider our options and consciously choose to act rather than be complacent with our lives as they are. By making mindful choices rooted in compassion, integrity, and ethics, we can help others, make our environment richer, and build positive karma for ourselves.

Past Lives Shaping Present Karma

Return of the Killer Karma

As we can see from the example of Pop-Pop being a great-grandfather to his own reincarnated descendant, Dylan, karma comes around in unexpected ways. We can never say when or where, but it certainly does influence us. When we consider the unresolved issues from past lives, the deeper the problems, the more impactful the consequences.

For instance, someone who faced a painful betrayal in a previous life might struggle with trust issues in their current relationships. Strong feelings of guilt or shame that might have no source within the current lifetime can lead to self-destructive behaviors. This hinders personal growth and fulfillment. Speaking from my own difficult experiences, this lingering lack of resolution can make you feel like life is spiraling out of your control. It took me years of soul-searching and professional guidance to find my way back up to the surface. It was a matter of isolating emotional and mental patterns and behavioral traits that cropped up in certain situations.

Here's another example: You might have acrophobia despite never having been in physical danger of falling from tall buildings or great heights. This does not diminish the fear. Instead, you and your support system must consider how the symptoms occur while carefully searching for the root of this fear. Recognizing these patterns can help you address and even heal these past wounds. This contributes to the resolution of your karmic debts while improving your quality of life. It's possible to accomplish this by building your self-awareness, working on your emotional strengths, and opening your mind to various holistic healing techniques.

Awareness Exercises

Certain techniques can help boost your instinctive ideation and further improve your ability to recollect past-life memories or sensations. This is not PLR, though, which is best conducted under the trained eye of a hypnotherapist. The few activities I suggest here are similar to the exercises from Chapter 3, which were to help you with PLR therapy. But these can aid you in gradually growing mindful of your consciousness in the present and, if luck is on your side, in the past as well.

- **Meditation:** Practice a daily mindful meditation. You can do this with a group, a partner, or on your own. Pay attention to your posture and the way every breath infuses your chest with life-giving air. It works best when you commit to it regularly and build a healthy attitude toward spending time on focused meditation techniques. This is when you set aside your phone and any work related to your home or job.

- **Journaling:** Keep track of your thoughts and ideas. As mentioned in the previous chapter, you will find clarity through this habit. Write about your day and see how much you can remember about how you felt during certain events. What I find personally striking about using a journal is that there is a difference between directly experiencing an event versus remembering it. Say a young employee, Betty, has a flat tire and needs to catch a bus to the office. She might arrive there late and start her work in a disgruntled mood. But in hindsight, Betty might realize that she appreciated the sights of the city from the bus in a way she can't enjoy when she drives herself to work every day. You never know when a situation might seem completely different simply by giving it some time!

- **Guided practices:** Along the same lines as PLR therapy, you can attempt other guided activities such as dream analysis, energy work, reiki healing, tarot card reading, and more. Do your research to find competent professionals in your area who can offer these services in a way that benefits you. Sometimes, certain practices may not suit your situation or thought process. That's alright. It's a matter of trial and error to find practitioners who are in tune with your needs. With the right guide, you can find new patterns and perspectives on your dreams, emotions, and state of mind.

The Past Affects the Present

It is easy to teach people that past actions from this life can influence our present because everyone has experienced this in some way. However, understanding that actions from past lifetimes can influence our current lives is a bigger deal. This idea is deeply philosophical and spiritual and easier to accept when we experience it for ourselves.

Ash Riley is an astrologer, science editor, marketer, and rational mystic. She has navigated expertly through the world of business, having worked as a journalist, entrepreneur, and business consultant. She understands the tech and money side of things as clearly as the spiritual side of the world. With her unique experience, Riley is outspoken against false advertising of wellness coaching, toxic spiritual teachings, and wrongful energy work. Instead, she uses her years of across-the-board training to find the best evidence-based research to customize her guidance to every client who works with her.

An avid believer in reincarnation and karma, Riley has dedicated her life to working in this area, helping people find resolution from their karmic debts. She focuses on the profound connection between past-life issues and their consequences in the present, as explained on her website, My Sacred Space.

One of Riley's friends struggled with low self-esteem, anxiety, and depression for years. She saw that his unexplained and debilitating pains were caused by traumatic incidents in his previous life. It affected his work visibly, and he gave up on his goals when he couldn't find the inner strength to pursue them, as she writes in a blog article titled "How Past Lives Affect Our Current Life" (Riley, 2021).

Riley referred this friend to a known distance healer, Tara, after seeing that he was leaning toward that direction. Faith is everything when it comes to energy work. With her friend believing that Tara could really target the source of his problems and help him, she managed it. It turned out that what he had was an energy blockage caused by unresolved issues from his previous incarnation. It was a buildup of his unrelenting negative emotions, which suppressed his inspiration and capacity to live his life to the fullest. He now understands that had he not sought out a proactive way to tackle the problem, he would have kept running into this issue.

Riley suggests that unresolved traumas or patterns from previous lives can manifest as emotional struggles or recurring challenges and problems. With this in mind, she encourages people to explore their connections and recognize the real cause of their challenges. The root is often buried in the past and not easily accessible. But when you start soul-searching and keep your mind open to new ideas, you can get further in life.

Lessons From Past Lives: Practical Applications

I like to believe that reincarnation gives us the chance to improve the karma we received at birth. It is, of course, a little more complex than that, but this idea can be a good starting point. It motivates us to do better and be better. We are thus in competition against ourselves. It is not a race against the people we coexist with but a healthy learning opportunity to figure out how to be even a smidge more decent than our past selves.

Learning From the Past

The best lessons are remembered when they come from emotionally strong experiences. This includes positive and negative situations where we can learn from past goodness and also take wisdom from failures.

Let's say somebody—we can name him John—believes he might have gone through hardship in a past life, a trauma that was never truly addressed. This can lead John to harbor certain ill feelings before he even remembers the exact situation that caused them. But if he chooses to look at it in a positive light, John can figure out how to settle his debt by showing empathy to people stuck in similar strife. By offering help to others in his current life, he begins to balance out his karmic debt and becomes a beacon of strength and hope in his community.

His actions are now about helping those in need, performing volunteer work, or simply being a more patient man with his friends and family. These behaviors improve him as a person, his situation, and his karma. John has used his effort to recognize that everyone has their battles and that it is a matter of choice and even luck to respond to the world with kindness rather than judgment. His patience with the people around him has allowed for better decisions and more consideration to be given to everyone rather than hurrying to get rid of an overwhelming problem.

These lessons of patience and resilience enforced by acts of kindness create a ripple effect from one man out into the world, thus showing how we can benefit from learning from negative situations from past lives. Such a thought process can inform our daily choices, help us be more mindful, and motivate us to act with intention.

Practical Improvements

Working on ourselves is tough but worth it. This is a lesson I repeat to myself regularly. Learn from my experiences and put these insights to good use. It's incredibly freeing to exercise your will to work on yourself. When you figure out certain past-life lessons, you can put your mind to it and improve yourself. Learn from failure and rejection. Be ready for good and bad possibilities. Preparation goes a long way.

For example, you can set personal goals based on your current self's experiences. After reflecting on what worked well and what didn't in previous difficult situations, create specific and relevant plans for managing impending concerns. Make sure your goals are achievable and that you take breaks to recharge while you're working toward them. This practice not only builds accountability but also shows a clear path to a solution. You can do this on your own, with a partner, or with a community where you involve each other, respect everyone's voices, and bring people together as you solve problems.

Of course, goal setting is part of your personal and professional growth journey. To ensure you stay on track, it helps to reflect on yourself regularly to see how you respond to your own ideas. Sometimes, a decision you make early on may seem lackluster several weeks or even years later. That only means you have gotten new information, grown, or feel differently about a situation. Leave room for adaptability and allow your soul to learn and grow even during a short project.

I would also suggest searching for a mentor. Have a guide who can discuss profound concepts with you while also encouraging you to try new feats based on your past-life memories. Often, you may feel overwhelmed without knowing why, but that might be because you faced severe obstacles in a certain area in the past. That's alright. Take a step back, consult with your mentor, and approach your target with a different strategy.

In the same vein, you can also try and mentor someone else. Reach out to a mentorship program where everyone receives and gives guidance in a spectacular circle of give-and-take. You can build a powerful community of open-minded believers who support you during difficult times and rejoice with you when you succeed.

Balancing Karma Across Lifetimes

Neutralize Negative Karma

I don't mean to make it sound like you're searching for the right wire to cut on a ticking time bomb. Many of us never know when our current life will end and the next one will begin. So, make the most of the time you have.

Negative karma is responsible for the karmic debt I mentioned earlier in this chapter. It can be neutralized in many ways, not least of which is showing gratitude to people. Even admitting that you are grateful has a positive impact. It shifts focus away from negative experiences and builds a sense of abundance that you might have never thought you had.

Keep a gratitude journal. Penning down specifically positive thoughts on the things you appreciate brings you into an optimistic cycle of thinking. Write about the things or people you are thankful for. Mention at least one item each day. You'll come to realize how much you have, and you won't fret as much about the things that are gone. Yes, mourn the losses, but don't forget to celebrate the wins as well!

Consider forgiveness. For many, this means giving people another chance to hurt others. That is *not* what I intend. Forgiveness improves your ability to accept attrition from people who have made mistakes and are willing to atone. It requires letting go of anger and dropping any grudge you may be holding.

Ask yourself why you feel angry. It is not a good or bad emotion; it just is. Anger is a form of protection. It tells you that you have been hurt, but you need not roll over and allow more hurt to happen. Up to a point, anger can help you and keep you going. It is equally important to know when to let it go.

It's not easy, I admit. But you can do it when you redirect your energy to what you want to build rather than what you wish to tear down. I suggest guided meditation practices, gentle breathing activities, and reflective exercises. A regularized routine will help improve your mood on a long-term basis and create a more positive mindset. This can even mitigate the lingering effects of past-life negativity and help you handle current-life hardships while working toward a more hopeful future.

When you're able to show gratitude and forgiveness, you can craft a personality with selflessness at its core. You can achieve positive karma through performing acts of kindness that benefit others without expecting anything in return. In fact, you feel an emotional boost from lending help to the people around you. A well-intentioned act can help your next-door neighbor. Perhaps you engage in mindful acts of service, whether through small gestures like holding the door open or offering a listening ear. In turn, that can build a clear path of kind acts from person to person. Their moods will be at an all-time high, and that becomes clear in their interactions. You might even receive their gratitude in due time, and this helps you as well. It is a positive feedback loop where everyone steps up and helps each other out.

In this manner, when you work to build positive karma, you help others do the same. It goes to show how improving your karma is never an isolated job. The effort is interconnected between people in a community and beyond.

Al-Danaf and Khaddage

Born in 1992, Nazih Al-Danaf was just over two years old when he told his parents that he used to be a bodyguard for the Dar El Taifeh (the Druze Center, located in Beirut) and had been killed in action in 1982. In his previous life, he had been Fuad Assad Khaddage. He'd been married twice and had eight children from his first marriage and five from his second. His widow, Najdiyah, was one of the first faces the young Nazih recalled when he told his new family about his past life.

Dr. Erlendur Haraldsson, a psychologist and professor emeritus at the University of Iceland, and Dr. James G. Matlock, an anthropologist and researcher, investigated the case thoroughly and were impressed with how many of the young boy's statements were verified by Khaddage's family. They documented how Nazih vehemently demanded to visit the right house and find Khaddage's wife and children. When the boy did, he found Najdiyah and her five children. He also met Khaddage's brother and set about telling everyone specific memories that shocked and impressed them.

The family believed that Nazih was Fuad Khaddage in a new form. He knew far too many things, especially details that nobody else could have known, for it to be coincidental.

Dr. Haraldsson and Dr. Matlock detail the account in their 2017 book, *I Saw a Light and Came Here*. They wrote, "Since that time the families occasionally visit one another. We observed affectionate embraces between Nazih and the family as we parted" (Harraldson & Matlock, 2017).

This is what caught me personally. When you read the book, you will also see it. The young child, Nazih, had been unrelenting at first, doing all he could to convince his family to visit the people of his past life. His mother, Naaim Al-Danaf recalled her son saying this at just 18 months of age: "My children are young, and I want to go and see them" (Harraldson & Matlock, 2017).

Nothing but unending love for his family even through death and rebirth could have given him that strength. Reuniting with his wife and children had been the goal all along. Despite having lost a dedicated father, Najdiyah's children found solace when Nazih returned to them.

Choosing Fate

I consider the above story a balance of karma across lives. It was not Fuad Khaddage's fault that he left his wife and children. But his soul did everything possible to make sure they were reunited. Nazih chose to act on this. He made the decision to go back and find his wife and kids. It was well worth the effort, especially now that all the families involved are on excellent terms with each other.

My first question about this idea of connecting karma with reincarnation had been to ask why it is necessary to consider this debt important. Actions done in a past life may or may not be remembered in the current one. So, why must we take it into account? Why should the responsibility be carried over even when the memories are not?

It is because we must address our own fates. Say someone—let's call her Jane—has a serious case of misfortune befall her. She has just broken up with a long-time partner and has been performing poorly at her job. She is facing probationary action and has to figure out how to buck up her work to avoid getting fired. This isn't so rare a situation. Anyone who has gone through enough of life knows that several bad things can happen at once. This tests our abilities to cope with all the issues we're managing, and we often drop the ball on some of them. Jane faces such a series of hurdles now. She knows that she might have handled them well if they'd shown up one at a time. But she can now exercise her free will to choose to help others and, by virtue of that, help herself access a better future.

Understanding that some poor decisions in the past have led to this inevitable hardship, Jane can find the silver lining she needs. If she perseveres and continues to do helpful and good deeds, she can change her future. And this is what I wish for everyone reading this book to really grasp. Reincarnation need not be the unending cycle it seems. We can use it to change our karma!

Of course, not everyone finds this easy to believe. Let's take a look at what many people assume and mistake about the concepts of reincarnation and karma. These skeptics raise real concerns, but can we pose rebuttals? I believe we can.

Chapter 5

Addressing Skepticism and Misunderstandings

I do not think scientists in other disciplines need lose anything except some of their assumptions—such as that a person is nothing but a physical body—if they examine open-mindedly the evidence we have of life after death. –Ian Stevenson

A nonbeliever might not even finish reading the above sentence before they scoff at it. But that is because they have made up their mind based on the evidence they have already seen and are unwilling to consider anything new or that doesn't fit into their ideas of life and death. And although we have more evidence-based case studies supporting reincarnation, they are still not as concrete as the objective, observable truths of the universe.

The Skeptic's Guide to Reincarnation: Addressing Doubts

Suspicion about reincarnation often stems from reliance on nonempirical data. This is challenging for many in the Western world, who prefer solely scientific methods. It's not illogical. I fully understand why evidence-based reasoning is prioritized. We can't just go about blindly trusting everything we read or hear about.

This is what critics argue about. They don't consider personal anecdotes genuine evidence because these accounts cannot be verified, standardized, or repeated in controlled conditions. The lack of tangible or measurable proof makes it difficult to accept any kind of paranormal phenomenon as legitimate. Without concrete proof of reincarnation, a solid majority of the population refuses to put their stock in it.

Skeptics also point out how psychological and cultural factors influence these beliefs. Yes, cases of past-life memories can be attributed to suggestion under hypnosis, imagination, or cultural conditioning. Now, while many false cases have been debunked with this perspective, that does not undermine the actual experiences of people who do remember their past lives.

Doubts and questions add layers of complexity to the argument. I don't believe there are just two sides to the situation. That there are believers and nonbelievers makes it more rounded and three-dimensional. It does us all an injustice to consider believers as gullible and nonbelievers as pessimists.

For and Against

Dr. Raymond Moody is an American psychiatrist, physician, and author. He hadn't been a believer in paranormal phenomena but still took it upon himself to search for data. From the start, he expressed an open-minded approach to exploring consciousness and the afterlife. As he progressed through his research, he came upon the concept of near-death experiences, where people sense their consciousness leave their mortal form for a precious few minutes during or after a life-threatening situation.

Dr. Moody also worked through PLR therapies and came to believe in the reincarnation cycle based on the memories he recalled after several deep sessions. Outlined in his book, *Coming Back: A Psychiatrist Explores Past-Life Journeys*, originally published in 1991, he explains his experience with regression hypnosis as conducted by his good friend and colleague, Dr. Diana B. Denholm, a notable psychotherapist. Dr. Moody writes (2017):

> I wanted to experience past-life regressions myself. I expressed my desire to Diana, who graciously offered to do a regression that very afternoon. She seated me in an overstuffed reclin-

er and led me, slowly and skillfully, into a deep trance. Later she said I had been under for about an hour. At all times I was aware of being Raymond Moody and of being under the guidance of a wonderful hypnotist. But at the same time, I went back through nine civilizations and was able to see myself and the world in many different incarnations. To this day, I don't know what they meant—or even if they meant anything. I do know that they were very intense experiences, more like reality than a dream. (p. 6)

Afterward, Dr. Moody developed an unwavering belief in rebirths. He might not have come to this conclusion had he not been open to varying stances and trying out new processes to explore the many unexplained phenomena in the world.

On the other side, we have Dr. Alex Lickerman, a famous doctor and founder and chief medical officer of ImagineMD, a primary health care facility in Chicago. He also used to hold the roles of director of primary care and assistant vice president for student health and counseling services at the University of Chicago. Trust me when I say that he's been around for a while and knows quite a bit when it comes to the field of medicine.

In his article "The Problem With Reincarnation," Dr. Lickerman clearly states that he does not believe in reincarnation (2012). He is, however, a Buddhist. Having studied the ancient texts on Buddhism deeply for years, Dr. Lickerman has seen the value in being part of this faith, but he does not see reincarnation as a viable possibility. At first glance, this sounds like a paradox because aren't those two aspects supposed to go hand in hand? But there's more to this, as he explains.

In the same article, Dr. Lickerman asks this interesting question (2012), "So when people tell me they believe in reincarnation, the first question that comes to my mind isn't about what evidence they think argues for the possibility. Rather, it's this: just exactly what do they think gets reincarnated?"

His point of view is food for thought. He iterates that Buddhism does not establish a soul as such. When I say "soul," I mean our consciousness, which is not corporeal but has been carried from life to new life ever since it was created eons ago. Buddhism does not see the soul as an indestructible essence that can exist between various lives without a body, as some may understand it. So, what is it that is reincarnated is what the good doctor asks.

I might not have a clear response for him, but that's okay. The point of this conversation isn't to arrive at a one-size-fits-all solution; it is to keep the conversation going. Perhaps, our descendants will come up with the right language that their descendants can use to figure out an answer. As of now, we can and must keep this discussion alive. I implore you to keep researching case studies, keep speaking up, and keep searching within yourselves for more possibilities than you were told you have.

One thing I really admire about Dr. Lickerman's article is that it's written with tact. Thanks to the respect figures like Dr. Stevenson and Dr. Lickerman offer to those with opposing views, we get to see gallant knights face each other with competence and the acknowledgment that the other is just as courteous. Now, that's an attitude worth promoting!

This allows other believers to use their energy to address Dr. Lickerman's points validly and not just to defend themselves or Dr. Stevenson. This is important to consider. A conversation about true reincarnation must not devolve into an attack-and-defense situation. State your points in a nonconfrontational manner. You will get more flies with honey than vinegar.

I believe this is the true takeaway from the global conversation. Have an open dialogue without attacking each other's views, encourage exploration of various perspectives, and conduct more research into the subject. The science of today is not the same as it was a century ago. I would say we should allow the same leeway to reincarnation studies. It might be beyond our understanding now, but who knows what humanity will learn in a hundred years!

Scientific Perspectives: Evidence and Limitations

Criticism and Review

Conversations and arguments put forward in white papers, articles, journals, and books lead to the development of new theories. They show the depth of research and peer-reviewed work that goes into publishing such documents. Meanwhile, criticism and reviews of these publications lead to more refined interpretations of the topic.

We've seen how the diligent work of Dr. Ian Stevenson brought him to various cultures across the world and led to him interviewing thousands of children and families about their recollections. Documenting these accounts was only a small part of his overall research. Dr. Stevenson dedicated his career to attempting to uncover a behind-the-scenes look at reincarnation. Some would say he got no further than noting down similar patterns of memory recollection, birthmarks, and the like. Many such cynics stick to this mentality without being open to discussion.

That is not the case with Dr. Jesse Bering. He is the head of the science communication department at the University of

Otago in New Zealand. An article of his in *Scientific American* caught my attention because it was by someone who did not believe in reincarnation who'd nevertheless taken the time and effort to read Dr. Stevenson's books to further his knowledge on the subject.

Dr. Bering writes in the article titled "Ian Stevenson's Case for the Afterlife: Are We 'Skeptics' Really Just Cynics?" (2013):

> More often than not, Stevenson could identify an actual figure that once lived based solely on the statements given by the child. Some cases were much stronger than others, but I must say, when you actually read them firsthand, many are exceedingly difficult to explain away by rational, non-paranormal means. Much of this is due to Stevenson's own exhaustive efforts to disconfirm the paranormal account. (para. 4)

Dr. Bering highlights that since Dr. Stevenson went to great lengths to debunk false cases and singularly document the real ones, it was hard to dismiss his research as fake. It helped that Dr. Stevenson did not add his spin on interpreting what these narratives meant. He stayed as impartial as possible, surveying the data and interviewing people to get firsthand accounts of plausible cases from children on various continents.

An impressed Dr. Bering admits that the research has convinced him to open his eyes to the peculiarities of the world, even if he does not believe in reincarnation yet. It's a matter of opinion for every reader to accept a certain degree of truth in Dr. Stevenson's brilliant work.

I think that's a good step. We must change notions to fit facts, and never the other way around. And while a few people might not consider these narratives facts, perhaps that is also a matter of opinion.

Congruence of Studies

Diverse disciplines such as psychology, history, neuroscience, anthropology, and cultural studies offer intriguing insights into the ideas surrounding reincarnation. I mentioned this in Chapter 2 under the section "Interdisciplinary Approaches." This congruence of various areas of study shows reincarnation as a layered idea that can be understood better when we take all these fields into account.

Psychology, for instance, explores the nature of memory, identity, and consciousness, which helps when we look into claims of past-life memories and sort out the false ones from the truths. Researchers in this field may investigate how memories are formed, stored, and recalled, as well as the psychological factors that could influence a single person's or a community's beliefs in reincarnation. I find it fascinating that highly acclaimed STEM researchers are intrigued enough by déjà vu and vivid dreams to warrant in-depth studies into these concepts to be thoroughly funded. In conducting these studies, psychologists can shed light on the complexities of human perception and how they might relate to concepts of past lives.

Neuroscience contributes to this discussion on reincarnation by examining the brain's role in shaping consciousness and personal identity. Advances in neuroimaging techniques allow us to study brain activity associated with memories and experiences. It gives us a new lens, allowing us to really see how different people process information in their brains. Some neuroscientists explore the idea of consciousness beyond the physical brain, leading to discussions about near-death experiences, unexplained memories, and even transcendental understandings of life and death.

Anthropology examines human societies and cultures. Experts can use their studies to look into the many interpretations of reincarnation, which vary across different cultures and communities based on their history and religion. Anthropologists study rituals and myths, among other practices related to death and consciousness, offering us a comparative idea of reincarnation.

The field of cultural studies analyzes the ways in which cultural and regional beliefs are formed and expressed. In terms of reincarnation, this field explores how media, literature, and art reflect and shape societal views on life after death. This lets us know how these beliefs influence identity and community.

Favorable and modern depictions of multiple lives encourage people to be less skeptical about the idea and even consider it more seriously.

Historical analysis can reveal how concepts of reincarnation have evolved within various civilizations. By examining ancient texts, artifacts, and historical accounts, historians can trace the development of reincarnation beliefs and their impact on societal norms, philosophies, and religious practices. I don't know about you, but when several tribes, dynasties, regimes, and civilizations across millennia believe in a concept, I would certainly take an interest in it as well!

The study of religion is an interesting lens on its own. It delves into the theological and philosophical foundations of reincarnation within various faiths, particularly Hinduism and Buddhism. Researchers examine sacred texts, doctrines, and religious practices about the cycle of life, death, and rebirth. In this manner, the literature of religious studies provides deeper insight into how these beliefs shape the moral understanding of reincarnation.

Altogether, these different disciplines give us incredibly diverse vantage points on the same concept, thus providing many deeper understandings of the cognitive and emotional aspects of human experience. It was the amalgamation of multiple studies that built Dr. Ian Stevenson's reputation, and that of many experts, to what it is today.

I believe it's essential to have a calm, critical, and open-minded approach when assessing reincarnation case studies. Consider these queries: How valid is the evidence you see? Are there alternative explanations for a person's unexplained memories?

If you endeavor to conduct your own studies, the quality of a narrative must be verified to the best of your ability. If you can verify the findings with a substantial body of evidence (checking facts with the people who knew the person in their previous life), then the account is more credible than vague visions.

Alternatives are some of the first points skeptics might ask about. So, they must also be the things we ask. Are there psychological or social factors that could explain a person's peculiar visions? We must figure out if they can be ruled out before claiming that the visions are memories of a past life.

Cultural Misalignments: Bridging Eastern and Western Perspectives

Mixed Reactions

As mentioned in Chapter 3 under "Rebirth in the West: Modern Tales of Reincarnation," we must clarify our definitions before charting our course. To reiterate what I stated earlier, a discussion on an Eastern understanding includes the cultures and religions based in Asia, Africa, and Oceania, while a Western perspective covers North and South America, most of Western Europe, and Australia.

Cultural backgrounds play a significant role in shaping a person's beliefs. We are moved by our community, and our community is built by us. For many, religion is indistinguishable from their region's culture and lifestyle, often going hand in hand with following moral practices and guidelines. For some, religion is a choice they make to find answers to the questions they have about metaphysical concepts of the universe. For some others, religion is not a factor in their lives, but they may still choose a kind of spirituality to hold on to. We are concerned with such different ideas within various populations who wish to find answers and peace in the lifestyle they have chosen.

In some ways, a percentage of the different populations I've mentioned exists in many parts of the world, whether in harmony with each other or not. Let me summarize what we discussed in Chapter 1: Traditionally, followers of Hinduism, Buddhism, Jainism, and surrounding faiths tend to view reincarnation as a fundamental part of the cycle of life and death. It influences moral behavior and life choices. In cultures with monotheistic religions such as Christianity, Islam, and Judaism, reincarnation is not the focus; instead, the Day of Judgment is where all our karma determines our final sentence.

Many of us tend to view Western practices as ideologies that scoff at reincarnation and true karma and Eastern faiths as

systems that uphold them. I think this is a vague general-
ization. A Christian can believe in rebirth and karma, as we
have seen with the understanding of the transmigration of
souls, a popular concept in orthodox practices of Judaism and
Christianity.

Similarly, a Buddhist can stand apart from the notion of reincarnation, as Dr. Alex Lickerman continues to do. Ultimately, it is down to what we understand from our cultures and
where we find meaning.

Can you sit down and discuss your ideas with someone who
does not hold your views? Can the both of you share a civil
conversation without poking holes in each other's faiths? We
must go beyond tolerance and strive for genuine acceptance.
The point of this book is not to help or encourage you to
convert people to this mode of thinking. It is to show the
world that a choice exists. Free will exists. You can affect your
karma. You can certainly learn new ideas, even if they relate
to something that you didn't believe before. But above all, it
is to show that we who do believe in reincarnation and karma
deserve to have as bright a stage as those who do not. Only
then will it be a fair and fulfilling debate.

Authenticity in Spiritual Teachings

Let's take medicine as an example. The most modern
form of medicine is derived from the Hippocratic sources
of research-based treatment. It has developed from sci-

ence-backed, tested biochemistry and feels like a far cry from various other forms of treatment and care. The modern version is also referred to as "the Western advancement of medicine." However, we never would have gotten here if we didn't have anything to go on from ancient teachings.

Turmeric has mild healing properties. Lavender has been used for anxiety-reducing and sleep medicines. Poppy was used in old pain relief concoctions. The long history of these treatments shows how various cultures used the plants around their communities to help and heal people for thousands of years. Until the advent of modern science, people didn't know the chemical composition of the medicines they ingested. Every formulation was built on trial and error by healers who used the resources around them and worked off of the knowledge from previous generations.

But when it comes to commodifying medicine, health practices, and religious identities, certain Western conventions have stood on the shoulders of Eastern traditions and claimed credit as the source. I suppose this is how karma has been misinterpreted on many Western media platforms. When people do not consider samsara and the reincarnation cycle, they tend to see karma as a cosmic force that punishes a wrongdoer and nothing more. Such thoughts can lead to a superficial understanding of these deep-rooted themes.

Karma isn't about personal branding or self-improvement, though it can help with these ideas. It is so much more, relating to everything from the interconnectedness of life to the moral implications of our actions beyond death. The true spiritual significance of reincarnation may be overshadowed or even lost when consumerism takes over.

When we consider true spiritual teachings, we must refer to the foundations of the original source. Adapting older versions of any philosophy is no easy task. Our Western interpretations of reincarnation have watered down the real deal, but that doesn't mean we must stop in our tracks. Go ahead and work your way back to the older texts. The internet has given us a wide world of data that's accessible at any time. You can do your own research and find first- and secondhand accounts of reincarnations that have been substantiated by a body of evidence. Follow the experts in the field and see if you can branch out onto your own path.

Common Misunderstandings: Clarifying Key Concepts

We've gone over how people can be skeptical about karma and reincarnation when they don't know exactly what these concepts entail. Let's now consider a few popular misconceptions about reincarnation and what people might get wrong about concepts related to it.

Reincarnation and Resurrection

The misunderstanding between these two terms might happen when we search for examples in the mythologies of different religions. Reincarnation occurs when, after death, your soul or consciousness moves on to another body for a new process of birth, life, and death. We've seen how this is the idea promoted by religions such as Buddhism and Hinduism. Resurrection is when, after death, the soul returns to the same body it left to bring it back to life. The most prevalent instance of this is Jesus Christ being resurrected three days after his sacrifice.

In short, reincarnation is the continuous journey of the soul, while resurrection is the reversion of death, allowing life to resume from where it was paused. This difference shows contrasting views on life after death, and they're quite varying perspectives of what rebirth entails, depending on your faith or spirituality.

Karma and Fatalism

You may have seen karma being misunderstood as fatalism. Perhaps some of you even thought of it that way before finding more information. For the rest of you, fatalism is the idea that we (people, animals, and all life on earth) are actually powerless to do anything other than what we do.

Yeah, sunny.

People have done their homework on the matter. Dr. Ricardo S. Silvestre published a paper titled "Karma Theory, Determinism, Fatalism and Freedom of Will" that looks into Eastern teachings of karma and tries to devise the connection between that and people's understanding of fatalism. As a decorated professor connected to the University of Brasília, the Federal University of Campina Grande, and the Federal University of Rio de Janeiro, he takes an empirical view. In his paper, he states (2017):

> The basic principles of karma theory, together with a couple of very simple logical and conceptual principles, do imply a sort of determinism, fatalism, and lack of free will. There is, however, some more to say about these principles. Despite their apparent individual intuitiveness, taking them together seems to trivialize the very notion of karmic effect. (p. 58)

When they mistake it as a theory of fatalism, people assume karma implies a lack of agency. But we've gone over this, and you now understand that karma is solely based on your actions. The lack of agency idea comes in because our actions have consequences in the next life, but we might never remember what we did to warrant the situation. It's easier to accept karma as a principle of cause and effect where good acts lead to good fortune and bad acts lead to bad fortunes, but it feels scary in practice.

That's why we must consider other people. When a friend has done something good in their previous life, their rewards can benefit us as well. It is the same when we consider ill-advised decisions or terrible deeds. Each person's karma can affect others, and that's where the idea of "resigning to fate" can pervade our lives. But we must not be resigned. Remember, karma encourages personal responsibility. No man is an island, and we are all connected through our deeds.

Karma in Modern Context: Relevance Today

We have always applied ancient teachings to our modern-day lifestyles. The mathematical theorem of Pythagoras and Euclid is still being studied and deconstructed. Philosophies, arts, and sciences of the ancient Greeks, Romans, Muslims, and Asians have been carried down the ages to form the basis of our current studies. There is always something to be understood from our ancestors and from grand and rich world history.

Knowing this, it is not out of the ordinary to incorporate classical or even bygone texts into our understanding. People of different cultures continue to follow the beliefs of karma today, adopting it as a principle to live life by. It helps to have some guidelines in a world where any action can lead to unforeseen but inevitable reactions. I find it comforting to know that there is a cosmic balance to our chaos and that we can influence this balance by ensuring our karma stays on the positive side. It's definitely one of the many things that helps me sleep at night.

Beyond just believing in it, we must live according to the guidelines. This often involves mindfulness and self-reflection, two acts that we shall cover in detail in the following chapter. Be aware of your actions and the intentions behind them. You can use meditation and yoga to build an optimistic attitude filled with compassion for yourself and others.

When people recognize that their actions—whether kind or harmful—can create a ripple effect, they may be more inclined to act with integrity, empathy, and responsibility. This is how abiding by the karmic theory shows me that we can work together and live in harmony. The practice builds a sense of accountability in each of us. Let's be mindful of the way our actions can impact our future lives and that of others around us.

Help people recognize the interconnectedness of all beings and the impact of their choices. Engaging in community service or acts of kindness reinforces this belief. Continue to be proactive. Consciously integrate karma into your routine and discover how you can change your world. In the next chapter, we will focus on these themes and see how to properly incorporate specific techniques to build a better future and a stronger karma for ourselves.

Chapter 6

Practical Karma: Applying Teachings to Daily Life

*Interestingly, believing in reincarnation and
an afterlife can contribute to lowering anxiety
around death.* –Mark Travers

F ear of death is common. The number of people who
have *not* had a brush with death tends to be greater
than those who have. But perhaps you have lost someone
close to you, a friend or a relative. The trauma of the passing would vary greatly, especially if you were able to mourn
them properly. However, the real fear, I believe, comes
from this: We don't know what happens after death. Not
for sure, anyway.

This is why I rely on being proactive. We will not be given the
answer; we must go out and set the foundation for the solutions. So, if the question is, "Do you know what happens after
we die?" then my response is this: I cannot give you a concrete

answer, but from my experiences, we have the chance to be reincarnated to settle our cosmic balance sheets—our karma.

And to be proactive, we must find ways to practice pragmatic routines to better our karma. I'm talking about being mindful of the fact that every action matters. Everything we do means something. A single mundane act can lead to or at least contribute to a wholesome and meaningful outcome. So, let's see how we can make this a reality.

Mindful Actions: Creating Positive Karma

Mindful actions refer to those in which we are fully present and intentional in our choices, considering the impact they have on ourselves and others. It's vital to build this kind of awareness in our daily interactions and decisions. I don't mean that we should do this just to fix our karma but also to become better people. This is how we align our actions with values such as compassion, kindness, and responsibility.

Personal and Transformative Growth

Merely understanding karma leads to a direct improvement in behavior. It reminds us that positive actions can lead to beneficial outcomes while negative actions can be harmful to ourselves or those we care about.

Mindfulness

Say somebody recognizes that their emotional outbursts have always hurt their family members and friends. It can be hard to curb such pain, but it's not impossible. With a little nudging, this person can seek professional support and therapy to work on their anger management and thus behave better toward the people they care about.

The reward for this change is that their family will be grateful, and their bonds will be stronger than before, as they have weathered the storm and come out victorious in the end. This awareness of cause and effect improves relationships and allows for growth as people consciously choose actions that support themselves and others. In this manner, we can identify certain patterns of positive and negative responses related to our actions.

Reflection

Reflect on your day. Consider what your intention behind certain memorable actions was. Were your acts motivated by kindness, a sense of responsibility, or less positive values? If you aren't entirely sure, consider the impact of your words or decisions on others. Did the actions benefit them more than yourself? That might help you figure out how you approached the situation.

Positive actions, however small, can serve as the seeds for transformative outcomes within a community. For instance, a quick smile directed at a sullen child can brighten their day. They might be in a better mood and less inclined to throw a temper tantrum at the grocery store. The parents can experience a swift and happy outing without dealing with an upset child. Their good temperament can lead to them helping out someone else by, say, holding open the door for them. As more people engage in these small acts—giving compliments, helping their neighbors, volunteering their time—the cumulative impact can build a more supportive community. Over time, small gestures of kindness can grow into larger acts of help.

Meditation Techniques for Karmic Awareness

You can take a break to try out these gentle exercises that help improve mindfulness and align your focus with the world.

Simple Techniques

Mindful Breathing

This seems so obvious, but it's really effective! Sit on a comfortable chair or your bed with your legs stretched out. Relax your body in a restful pose and begin.

1. Inhale slowly through your nose for five seconds.

2. Hold for eight seconds.

3. Exhale through your mouth for five seconds.

Repeat this for a few minutes, focusing on every breath. If your mind wanders, gradually bring your attention back to your breathing. Incorporate the technique into your daily routine, as this practice anchors you in the present moment and helps you develop awareness and patience.

Journaling

Write about the things you do and the thoughts behind those actions. When you set aside some time every day, you create a peaceful space to slow down and pay careful attention to your thoughts and ideas. Say you went shopping in the morning. Although it may seem insignificant, writing about it lets you know the value of menial habits and the substance in everything you do. The act of writing helps you process this and empowers you in the belief that your actions matter because you matter.

By writing every day, you begin to connect the pieces and see signs in hindsight. That plastic wrapper you left on the floor on Monday may have had ants gathering around it on Thursday. The incidental routine you have of leaving your towel on the floor after every shower has ensured that it's constantly wet. I offer mundane examples because these are what many of us likely become aware of once we start journaling.

The smallest of concerns suddenly stand out and reveal your personality in a different light altogether.

You can build this habit into a gratitude journal, as I brought up in Chapter 4. For example, if you write about a moment when someone helped you, you might reflect on the importance of being thankful and showing appreciation to them. In this way, you keep track of recurring instances of kindness and gratitude. It shapes your mentality into a more optimistic one and brings positive karma into your life.

Mindful or Conscious Walking

I don't mean to say that unconscious walking is a thing (unless you count sleepwalking). However, actively choosing to focus on the action of walking is a strong technique. Here, you are not walking to reach a destination. The goal is movement. With every step, you are aware of how your body moves and accommodates this constant motion to benefit your muscles, breathing, and the blood pumping through your veins.

Whether it's a walk in nature, a stroll down the lane, or taking your dog for an outing, making this activity a part of your routine helps keep your mind calm and your body active.

Professional Techniques

Guided meditation can be a powerful tool for exploring karmic patterns. The following techniques are best practiced under the guidance of professional therapists and experts on the subject of meditation. With years of training under their belts, they can take you through the motions carefully and surely, helping you find peace and clarity.

Visualization

When it comes to guided imagery, the exercise is best done with a certified therapist and as part of cognitive behavioral therapy. Your therapist or counselor will help you concentrate on the energy in your body. But this technique is quite easy to understand, so I have given you a sample here.

You begin by sitting or lying down comfortably. Close your eyes and take several deep breaths to relax as far as possible. The expert will speak gently and slowly so that you can listen at a comfortable pace. They will help you paint a picture in your mind using a strong metaphor.

Say the metaphor focuses on your relationships. Your therapist might help you imagine a fork in the road. You will need to choose to prioritize certain people above others, depending on the situation. For example, if your child is sick, a work meeting or school alumni gathering might have to take a back seat. If you have a promotion coming up, you'll perhaps need to have your partner or a babysitter take care of the kids more often. There is no universal right or wrong answer. Visualization helps you figure out the kind of thinking that will help you in these specific situations.

Remember, your therapist is not suggesting the answers for you. In fact, they will nudge you to figure out what the options are. They may suggest ideas such as, "Sink into the scene and experience it fully. Your visualization is more than simply a picture. This landscape represents your situation. Describe it. Take note of the paths you can access and the ones you cannot. Let's discuss them."

This process can help reveal the underlying energy blocks and karmic ties that are important to your current life. Exploring them in a safe environment is vital and might even take several sessions with a competent professional. No matter the case, do your best to approach it with an open mind.

Body Scan Meditation

Strictly speaking, we can do a body scan meditation on ourselves, but I have found better results with a guide who understands the stress and energy in our bodies. Essentially, this is how you go about practicing a routine body scan meditation:

1. Sit or lie down in a comfortable pose and close your eyes. Take a few moments to breathe deeply to relax your body and mind. All through the exercise, ensure you inhale and exhale deeply and slowly. Avoid moving your body too much during this time.

2. Start by gently bringing your awareness to your head. Avoid focusing too hard—it is a serene but firm

mindfulness you must exercise.

3. Notice any sensations or tension present in your head. Slowly, bring your focus down your face, along your neck, and into your shoulders. It may feel as though you are pulling the discomfort from your head downward into your body.

4. Gradually move your focus further down from your shoulders into your upper and then lower arms. Bring the weight of your discomfort through your hands and dispel it from your fingertips.

5. Come back to your chest. Focus on this area again and bring the weight down your torso and stomach, finally resting at your hips.

6. Continue going down, lowering your focus to your thighs, calves, shins, and feet. Let go of the stress and feel it leave through your toes.

This technique is remarkably effective for releasing physical tension. It also connects you to the deeper sensations and emotions in your body. After every scan, take a moment to reflect on any feelings or insights that arose during the activity. Your awareness of your body will grow as you build a routine of practicing body scans regularly.

Global Studies on Meditation

I would like to refer to the collection of over 450 studies conducted worldwide over the course of nearly 50 years that have focused on examining the benefits of guided meditation on various groups of people (David Lynch Foundation, 2023).

The compilation was drafted by Dr. Norman Rosenthal, an eminent psychiatrist and senior researcher attached to the Georgetown University School of Medicine and the National Institute of Mental Health. Accessible on the David Lynch Foundation site, the hundreds of papers published by several independent universities and research institutions show how people can work through their trauma and find solace from it using consistent meditation techniques.

The synopsis is based on decades of work and research on educators, veterans, abuse survivors, prison inmates, cancer patients, substance abuse patients, health care workers, and young adolescents, among others. The results show how long-term, regular, and focused meditation increases the chances of reducing traumatic symptoms and builds a clearer path to living life.

Try it out for yourself. Find what works best by exploring the various meditation techniques available. It can be a simple breathing exercise, yoga, or transcendental meditation. No matter your choice, ensure that you practice it daily. Immerse yourself in the activity and see how it helps nurture your awareness. Indeed, you'll find greater love and care for yourself and others. Using such compassion-focused practices, you can learn to forgive yourself and build your courage in the face of hardship, both in this life and the next.

The Art of Letting Go: Releasing Negative Karma

Letting go and forgiving are hard-won achievements. But with some guidance, practice, and care, you can make it look like a graceful art.

The Logic Behind Letting Go

Holding onto resentment gives temporary satisfaction but does not help us in the long run. Grudges can also cause deep stress and affect our emotional well-being. For example, we often loathe others for the pain they cause us or the success that they seem to have but we don't, despite the fact that we, too, have worked hard for it. Letting go of grudges and resentment brings us to a place of vulnerability. It is this space that frightens many of us, and for good reason. Forgiving ourselves or being free of the ache leaves us floundering in our emotions, which can feel raw and like too much to deal with all at once. But when we learn to figure out intense feelings and gather our thoughts, we can fare better in difficult situations.

It's a process that can strengthen interpersonal relations since forgiveness encourages empathy and understanding. It helps you develop strong and positive karma, bringing a more positive outlook on life that makes it easier to focus on your growth and happiness.

Clarity Against Resentment

Several notable people have found their paths in life by focusing on the positive results of letting go of negativity and pursuing more constructive approaches. We can learn how to live according to their teachings, such as those of Desmond Tutu. He was a South African Anglican bishop and a human rights activist who advocated against apartheid for several decades. But he did so by promoting forgiveness and reconciliation, emphasizing that letting go of past grievances was essential for healing. He lived his life following the principles of peace and nonviolence, and his words continue to reach out to millions of people around the world. He writes this in one of his many remarkable books, *No Future Without Forgiveness* (1999):

> Anger, resentment, lust for revenge, even success through aggressive competitiveness, are corrosive of this good. To forgive is not just to be altruistic. It is the best form of self-interest. What dehumanizes you inexorably dehumanizes me. It gives people resilience, enabling them to survive and

emerge still human despite all efforts to dehumanize them. (p. 29)

Deciding to take a stand and tackle the challenges that lie ahead works wonders for your karma. This practical and proactive stance helps you ward off some chances of negative karma and steers your choices toward creating or maintaining a positive but realistic environment. So, choose to be aware of your presence. Practice mindful breathing and other exercises. Take the time for self-reflection by journaling. These actions help you identify and change negative patterns in your life, thus freeing you from the harmful attributes of jealousy, resentment, hate, and negative karma.

Cultivating Compassion: Enhancing Karma

Positive Feedback Loop

We've seen how meditation and relaxing activities can calm the mind and energize the body. Strong positivity enhances our temperament and reduces stress symptoms. When we grow more patient toward ourselves, we can extend the same compassion to others. It leads to increased sympathy and improves the mood of the people around us. When they acknowledge the powerful ambiance we create, they reflect that strength back at us and the community around us.

Whether it's serving meals at a local shelter, mentoring youth, participating in environmental clean-up efforts, or feeding the local stray animals, these activities accomplish a lot. They address the immediate needs of the various lives we come across and also encourage a mindset of generosity and empathy.

As we demonstrate kindness, we become more attuned to the needs of others. These acts of service, in turn, generate feelings of fulfillment and connection, which can motivate further meditation and compassionate actions. Acts of kindness enhance personal well-being and contribute to a more understanding environment where kindness and helpful karma flourish. They reinforce the practical idea that good treatment builds healthy emotions, which contributes to positive behavior and yet more good treatment of others. This positive feedback loop can extend outward to impact our community.

Yousafzai's Karma

Many of us know the story of Malala Yousafzai. She is an incredibly brave and thoughtful activist who fights for the fundamental rights of children, girls, women, and people of color. In 2012, she was shot by the Taliban, but Yousafzai, who had been targeted for her outspoken strength, miraculously survived the assassination attempt.

After her arduous recovery, she gained a following of people from across the world who recognized her hard work and diligence. Her country came to support her ideas of peace and equality, as did the international community. Yousafzai was awarded the Nobel Peace Prize for her selfless behavior and courage in the battle to uphold the rights of the downtrodden. She was also invited to study in Birmingham in the UK, where she graduated from secondary school and later from university with her bachelor's degree. She is now the youngest recipient of an honorary fellowship at Linacre College, a constituent college of the University of Oxford. Karma certainly has done her well.

Yousafzai's courage in the face of terror stands the test of time. She gained recognition for her actions and is now a household name. She has taught us that a young girl's bravery can change everything and bring hope to millions of people worldwide.

Karma Yoga

No, it's not literally yoga. "Karma yoga" is the phrase we use to describe the path of taking intentional action without being too attached to receiving anything in return. Mentioned in the *Bhagavad Gita* by one of the most proactive characters, Krishna, it means a person can seek to achieve moksha (liberation) by performing specific good deeds to improve their karma.

I quite like this concept because it offers us a practical option to address our karma and eventually lift ourselves out of the reincarnation cycle. It's also not a mere theory but plausible, actionable advice. It is a regular spiritual practice of selfless service that encourages us to perform good deeds every day.

Like yoga, this attitude will help when it is enacted consistently, with all your heart and mind focused on the tasks. Build your mindfulness with every compassionate act and watch as you change your life and the world around you. Start small and work on yourself, picking up helpful habits that benefit you and the people around you. Soon, your routine will include performing a kind act every day without expecting a reward for it.

Practice Compassion

Whoever said it costs nothing to be kind did not understand the true weight of kindness. It always costs us something. It might take time away from you to pause your walk and help someone find directions to the subway. You might miss a cab if you help your new neighbor who is just moving in. It can cost a few bucks to get a decent bottle of water for someone who doesn't have a penny to their name. But it certainly helps them. In fact, it benefits them far more than it might cost you!

Try out daily affirmations to encourage yourself to perform certain acts of kindness. Set a reminder to check in on your elderly neighbor a couple of times a week. It may seem like an insignificant action, but it probably means the world to them. Practicing simple, small, and compassionate acts on a regular basis incorporates consistent kindness into your routine. It will become second nature for you to show goodness to others.

This helps counteract the obvious. Negative karma can accumulate throughout your life and cause serious havoc for you and others around you. It may feel desolate to consider that we must deal with the consequences of our previous lives; however, taking responsibility and being kind and courageous are brave acts. As Malala Yousafzai's actions illustrate, compassion can lead to positive outcomes. This reinforces the idea that our actions have a significant impact on the world around us.

This idea seems intuitive but is quite difficult to put into practice. Being weighed down by negative thoughts and emotions can change your psyche and make you feel as though you can gain clarity from holding onto grudges. It is difficult but worth the effort to unlearn this harmful attitude and embrace genuine care and forgiveness.

So, here I am, acknowledging that it takes a decent amount of effort to be kind. Yes, you deserve to be recognized for your compassion, but don't let it be the reason you help others. Allow yourself to rejoice along with them. Even if it is just for a moment, enjoy the lightheartedness that comes with guiding others on their journey. You help yourself as much as you help them. Your good karma shines with the effort and sacrifice you infuse into your actions.

Everyday Karma: Simple Practices for Daily Life

As I've emphasized above, it's important to develop a regular habit of performing good deeds and practicing compassion. This is how you can transform your routine into a helpful and productive one that benefits everyone. You can implement these gentle practices to improve your quality of life and find more fulfillment in the same activities you always do:

- **Practice mindful eating:** Take the time to savor your meals. Appreciate the flavors, textures, and effort that went into preparing your food. This will help you appreciate the food and the maker of the meal. If you cooked it yourself, you will value the work you put in.

- **Limit complaints:** Perhaps you have a constant stream of objections in your head. Unless something is life-threatening, see if you can lessen the criticisms. Challenge yourself to go a day without complaining. This helps shift your focus to more positive thoughts and interactions.

- **Volunteer:** Offer your time or effort to local charities. Helping others can create a ripple effect of positivity. Such acts of kindness can build connections between strangers and construct a stronger community.

Offer Gratitude

Start each day by listing three things you are grateful for. This helps you consider what you have waiting for you, either at work or home. If you have to undertake a mountain of tasks, then having enough time is something to be thankful for. If you have a deadline at the office, you might be grateful to your team for their work and contribution in helping you meet it.

It also helps to show gratitude. Strong, positive recognition for small and grand acts of kindness is a form of communication. When your baker offers an extra pastry with your purchase or a car slows down on the road to let you cross the street, show your appreciation. Give them a nod and a smile. When people express sincere thanks, it can lead to more constructive conversations and strengthen relationships. This is the sort of positive exchange that boosts karmic outcomes. I've said it before, and it's worth repeating that real acts of kindness and gratitude inspire others to reciprocate.

You can also bring this attitude into your journaling. We've gone over the benefits of this practice, and they're similar here. End the day by writing out what you felt grateful for. This helps build a positive mindset for future endeavors, helping you be hopeful about the possibilities. For example, if you write about a moment when someone helped you, you might reflect on the importance of being thankful and showing appreciation to them. In this way, you keep track of recurring instances of kindness and gratitude. It shapes your mentality into a more optimistic one and brings positive karma into your life.

When people engage in mindful actions, they are more likely to act thoughtfully rather than react impulsively. It helps lead to choices that nurture positive relationships and contribute to the well-being of communities. This intentional approach not only builds personal growth but also generates positive karma. Our mindful choices of today can yield beneficial outcomes tomorrow. By understanding the connections between our actions, we can create a ripple effect of positivity that enriches everyone's lives.

Karma helps us understand the actions that are considered right versus those that are wrong. It teaches us how our presence influences the world around us. This kind of self-reflection can aid in breaking negative patterns, balancing bad karma, and encouraging actions rooted in awareness and intention.

I believe that every human has some sense of self-preservation. We cannot always be completely altruistic. That's okay. As long as we try our best to be kind and genuinely helpful, it counts. Keep checking on yourself. Look back on your day and find out what you learned from the experiences and how you might approach a similar situation differently in the future. This consistent awareness of your actions can become a part of your daily routine. It's how you become a better person without competing with someone else for the rewards of life. Simply work at being a better you.

Chapter 7

Building Community and Spiritual Connection

When you plant a seed of love, it is you that blossoms. –Ma Jaya Sati Bhagavati

This is a wonderful quote from *The 11 Karmic Spaces: Choosing Freedom From the Patterns that Bind You* (2011). In the book, Ma Jaya Sati Bhagavati elaborates on her distinctive understanding of karma and interpersonal relationships. She delves into how our experiences and connections shape our spiritual journey. Her powerful words teach us how these aspects emphasize the link to mindfulness and compassion, which connect us to other people and the cosmos. Meditation, reflection, and community engagement can nurture this connection.

Throughout this book, I've emphasized my belief that by showing compassion and gratitude and being practical about our karma, we can build sincere interconnectedness among our people. The community will recognize how one person's actions can impact several others, including themselves. I believe this awareness can spark compassion and support among all of us, help us develop a strong spiritual connection with our karma, and help us build a real path to how we must live life.

Role of Sangha

Sangha, in the most foundational understanding, is a Sanskrit word for community. In the context of Buddhism, it refers to a group of practitioners who support each other on their spiritual journeys. The concept originated with the followers of the Buddha, initially consisting of monks who dedicated their lives to following and practicing his teachings. Later, this concept expanded to include nuns and other practitioners, called *bhikkus*, who were looking to create a supportive network that helped guide and teach each other ways of ethical living.

As I see it, the concept of sangha's strength lies in the communal aspect. The importance of collective practice and mutual encouragement builds more durable motivation than individual strength.

Support and Accountability

A sangha offers a supportive safety net and inspiration for everyone in the group. This is a circle of people who set out to follow the guidelines of the dharma, just as you have. By propping each other up during spiritual challenges, the group emboldens each individual. When one person faces difficulties, they are able to find guidance, discuss options, brainstorm with others, and seek direct help. This builds emotional strength, resilience, and the knowledge that we are not alone on our journeys. Continuous learning and collective wisdom ensure that any discoveries one person makes can be shared with the group, strengthening everyone. Every member can collaborate as much as they wish to and also benefit from the help of others.

Sometimes, the best way to learn is to teach! Teaching also deepens the sense of accountability because you know that you might be responsible for certain practices or knowledge that others can learn from you. This open collaboration motivates everyone to uphold their values and work toward improving their positive karma.

Find or Found a Sangha

Depending on your community resources, organizations close to you, your geographical location, and your culture, you can search for a sangha online, locate a group in your neighborhood, or even establish a community of like-minded individuals yourself. Attend local meditation groups or spiritual meetups. They might not be particularly religious or Buddhist—it differs from group to group. You can find suitable gatherings in community centers, religious houses, wellness studios, local gyms, or even online platforms and forums on verified websites.

As understood by the Thich Nhat Hanh Foundation (n.d.):

> The past is finished and the future is uncertain, only in the present can we discover the miracle of life. Living in this spirit, we are already valuable members of our Sangha. We will know how to engage in the continuous process of building a refuge for many beings. (Start a Sangha, para. 3)

Immerse yourself in these settings to obtain a shared experience. You can also build a supportive network that takes your views into account. Such an initiative empowers you to search for that sense of belonging in your community. You'll need to set aside some time, energy, and possibly funds to pursue this endeavor.

Find people who are ready to share your vision and go on similar spiritual journeys. You can start with a handful of others who would love to meditate together and try various mindfulness exercises. Sometimes, the simplest activities offer the best bonding opportunities. Take a walk in a park as a small group, for example. Use the buddy system so that you don't crowd the walkways. Enjoy the scenery, fresh air, green trees, open space, and the company of your people.

Personal Transformation

Brother Chye Chye talks about his experience being part of a sangha, where he found people with whom he could place his trust and confidence. As a banker with an engineering degree, his foray into the world of spiritualism transformed his outlook on life. While being interviewed by Cheryl from Handful of Leaves, he talks about how finding refuge in a sangha has an internal and external level. The external is to join the community, find solace, exude confidence, and also help uphold the teachings of the sangha. When it comes to the internal level, Brother Chye Chye says (2024):

> Internal Refuge the Sangha, what does it mean? It's about having that confidence in ourselves that one day we can be purified to become the ideal Sangha. So from external, it must come to internal. That's why the Buddha said that, you know, in the Parinirvana Sutta, he said mendicants or bhikkhus, be an island onto yourself. Be your own refuge. (Handful of Leaves, 4:16)

By immersing himself in the teachings and practices of Buddhism, Brother Chye Chye discovered a profound spiritual connection within his Buddhist sangha and its emphasis on mindfulness, compassion, and community.

The supportive environment of the sangha guided and encouraged him to explore his inner self. It's not easy to understand the principles of impermanence and interconnectedness. But Brother Chye Chye is well on his way to learning more than what the sciences have taught him. It's a lesson that benefits anyone willing to try.

Resources for Spiritual Growth

Searching for the right sangha can feel daunting when you don't know where to start. That's alright. Both online and offline resources can help you narrow it down to the right groups that will help you find what you're searching for. For example, Cornell University has a website that elaborates on their campus sangha community. Cornell is trustworthy thanks to their reputation, so this website seems more reliable than an unknown name.

You'll need to do your research. Check articles, videos, and newsletters that explain what the various communities offer you. Look into local workshops and retreats that host guided meditations. Places with good repute that offer immersive experiences for people to practice hands-on meditation and guided teachings are a boon to visit. Therapists who have guided you through deep meditation might also have excellent resources for you to explore.

Check out these links to see which sangha communities look promising:

- Cornell University: https://cornell.campusgroups.com/sangha/home/

- USA Sangha Council: https://www.usasangha.org/p/about.html

- Thich Nhat Hanh Foundation: https://thichnhathanhfoundation.org/local-communities-sanghas

- Brooklyn Zen Center: https://brooklynzen.org/

- Myosenji Buddhist Temple: https://nstmyosenji.org/myosenji2024/

- The Village Zendo: https://villagezendo.org/

You can also start with meditation practices at home by following tutorials and recitations from acclaimed priests and therapists. The online world has much to offer, but you can start by looking up these channels to see what piques your interest:

- Garchen Meditation Center: https://www.youtube.com/channel/UCJIep9LEmY1stCUKOenve_A/playlists

- Guhyasamaja Buddhist Center: https://www.youtube.com/user/GuhyasamajaCenter/playlists

- Ananda Sangha Worldwide: https://www.youtube .com/@AnandaWorldwide/playlists

Overall Safety

The usual cyber security concerns apply. I'm sorry to say that some places can and have fooled people into paying through money or effort. Whether you scour the internet or travel the roads to search for the right communities, remember that you should always put safety first! These simple tips can help keep you on track and boost your enthusiasm while staying aware of the fraudsters out there.

- Be careful when you conduct your research. Find reviews and testimonials to check if the groups are legitimate or scams.

- Start searching with the guidance of someone trustworthy, say a priest or rabbi you are acquainted with.

- Don't share private details of your life and family, especially information related to your money, health, and banking. There might be a registration fee for joining certain communities, but be careful if they start asking for more.

- Attend the first few meetings with a friend or partner to make sure you have found a good space where you can gain real support and also contribute.

You can find more resources when you find the right organization and ask the right forums online. People who are on the same journey as you will help out because they know as well as you do that it's a lifelong quest to search for clarity in this crowded and noisy world of ours.

Interfaith Dialogue: Embracing Diverse Beliefs

We have more than eight billion people on this lovely blue marble. It is simply not possible for all of us to follow a single line of thought, a sole religious identity, or a universal culture. Every one of us has a unique mind, heart, and soul. Many of us can band together under the banner of a single faith, but even that can branch out into several ideologies based on geography, race, gender, sexuality, and more.

This diversity must be celebrated. Such intrinsic and varied spiritual ideas show how every single person is capable of level-headed thinking and imagination. When it comes to concepts such as karma and reincarnation, it becomes even more mind-boggling to realize that we may have once been another mind, a different body, and a distinct heart in a land thousands of miles away. We might have been someone else with the same layer of complexity as we have now.

Positive Procedure

A clear procedure will remind people that everyone in the sangha has gathered to find direction, solace, and answers. Despite coming from various walks of life, each member will be able to connect and share their ideas by being compassionate and accepting of others.

Ensure you follow a helpful protocol when gathering in a community meet-up or sangha. Take note of these directions:

- **Set ground rules:** It helps to establish certain guidelines before you get started. For example, respectful dialogue and constructive advice function better than critical ideas.

- **Make a safe space:** Create a helpful environment for everyone to express their thoughts without fear of judgment. It's important to have an understanding of various backgrounds so that people of different strokes can mingle without worry.

- **Effective communication:** Practice empathy and active listening to ensure conversations benefit everyone involved. A dialogue must not be about who can speak louder than the rest. Proper communication allows everyone to add their voice to the discussions.

- **Following up:** This is subtle but quite effective. If a conversation is interrupted or if time runs out when someone is speaking, make a note of it and bring up that topic with the person the next time everyone gathers. This allows them to finish their explanation and encourages people to share their ideas despite limitations.

It's one thing to read about people of various religions, races, and ethnicities, but it's a completely different track to meet and talk to them. Be aware of cultural considerations and understand that while we do not have to learn every nuance, it is still wonderful to recognize and appreciate our differences. Share your spiritual experiences and give everyone a chance to take the floor and share theirs. Respecting everyone's turn is as important as recognizing the value of our differences.

Participate and Learn

You may have heard of interfaith conferences even if you haven't participated in any. Events that celebrate various religions and practices, such as these, are a great place to see how people from different places and cultures practice their faiths. Engaging with them brings up rich discussions that can provide you with new perspectives and help deepen your appreciation for the complexities of faith.

Perhaps you are Christian and believe in past lives. A conversation with a Buddhist can bring out so many unexplored ideas of reincarnation that could benefit both of you. Or you might be gnostic and eager to know more about the theories different religions have about karma and its influence on our lives. By immersing yourself in interfaith dialogues, you get to contribute to this melting pot of knowledge. You can also enrich your own spiritual journey by updating or adding ideas to those you previously believed in.

Sometimes, adventure does not knock on your door and lead you out into the world. You must put on your boots and start walking, ready to make your own journey. Life might not hand you a glowing invitation. But that's no reason to stay put in your comfort zone. Choose to explore! Embrace this chance to participate in powerful connections. There is beauty in the meeting of people that can be admired from any angle.

Cultivating a Supportive Environment for Spiritual Exploration

The right environment shapes the way you explore your spirituality. Say you have the undeniable support of your family and friends. This ensures your journey is open, free, and limitless. Your exploration is capable of helping you gain emotional encouragement and a sense of belonging. But if your relatives were to mock any kind of spiritual curiosity, their attitude could force you to hide your endeavors and put up walls against them. So, the journey would probably still happen, but it would be without the freedom and support of your family and friends.

Solo Space for the Soul

But you can still do your best to build a safe space for your practices. If you wish to develop a regular routine on your own, try out these tips:

- **Quiet space:** Designate a specific room or area in your home for your spiritual practice. Avoid working, studying, or lounging about in this place as much as possible. This space should be free from distractions and noise, allowing you to focus inward. It can become a good space for meditation, prayer, journaling, or reflection in general.

- **Natural light and plants:** If possible, have your meditation zone in a well-ventilated area that receives sun. This environment can lift your mood and build your quiet connection with nature. Your body will make good use of the vitamin D, and your chest will feel light thanks to the fresh air. Having plants in the room can do the same since green leaves can bring a sense of vitality and serenity to your space.

- **Calming elements:** You can improve the ambiance of your space by adding elements that benefit your mind and body. For example, some people like scented candles or incense; others prefer soothing music, white noise, or the sounds of rain playing in the background while they meditate. Choose the sensory aspects wisely since we all gravitate toward different elements.

Communal Space for the Soul

If you find a sangha or an offline forum where like-minded people are on similar spiritual paths as you, it might feel like coming home. Even workplace and community gatherings can impact your practice simply by virtue of providing proper support. When you find an opportunity to join any of the below initiatives, try it out! You might end up enjoying it more than you expect.

- **Spiritual groups:** Join or arrange a local group of people who are focused on sharing spiritual practices and contribute to open discussions on topics you are keen on.

- **Workshops or retreats:** You can engage in community workshops or retreats that focus on spiritual growth. Find a cohesive group of believers or even friends who are eager to try out new experiences. These events often promote deep connections and improve your mindfulness in meditation and other learning experiences.

- **Service projects:** You can join projects that align with your spiritual values as part of community service. Work with volunteer teams for a common cause and find how manual labor and spatial awareness of nature can fill you with a sense of purpose and fulfillment.

- **Support network:** By trying out various spiritual groups, retreats, and community service projects, you begin to build a network of friends and community members who share your zeal for spiritualism. This support system can enhance your personal experience while also creating a strong external space with other people.

The Importance of Continuity in Spiritual Practice

I've maintained that developing a routine has a real impact on our bodies, minds, and souls. Jogging once is good. Jogging every day makes a healthy difference. Smoking once is bad. Smoking every day is a death sentence for many. Trying a yoga pose is pretty good. Practicing yoga every day is what will help us develop a strong awareness of our bodies and improve our mindfulness and health.

Continuity is how a routine can influence us. This is the same for spiritual practice. Daily meditation, prayers, or mindfulness activities are essential for a serious and soulful impact. The consistency creates a rhythm that benefits us deeply. It helps reinforce the habits that support spiritual growth, making it easier to navigate life's challenges with a grounded perspective. You essentially commit to being a better version of yourself by regularly practicing these exercises.

Build a Routine

If you have had trouble developing or changing a routine in the past, try out these ways to incorporate a session for spiritual practice into your day.

- **Set a specific time:** Include a dedicated time in your daily schedule for spiritual activities. Avoid thinking of these as optional or additional activities. Whether it's an hour in the morning or the evening, make sure your priorities include this time for meditation or prayer.

- **Set alarms or reminders:** You can use your phone clock or an app to set daily reminders. Select a catchy tune to prompt you to finish up your current chores and settle down for your hour of meditation or any other mindful, spiritual activity.

- **Develop self-discipline:** Convince yourself to commit to this routine. Sometimes, people might have "cheat" days to allow themselves the luxury of not having to complete a task. But you must not think of your hour of meditation as a thankless chore. Remind yourself that this is an activity that you want to do with all your heart! Cheat days thus become meaningless because why would anyone skip an activity they enjoy?

- **Have a support network:** Ask a friend, a partner, or your sangha group to keep you on track. Sometimes, meditating with someone will help you feel less forced to accomplish the task and more eager to do it.

Hugh Jackman's Interview

You know of Hugh Jackman; we all do. He's one of the world's most pre-eminent movie stars of the century. He's the cream of the crop, the top brass, and has banged elbows with the best in the movie industries across the globe.

Dr. Norman Rosenthal, author of the book *Super Mind: How to Boost Performance and Live a Richer and Happier Life Through Transcendental Meditation* (2016), interviewed the star regarding his transformation and understanding of transcendental meditation. You can find a part of the interview on Oprah Winfrey's website.

Hugh Jackman admits to having been inquisitive and constantly searching for answers in the world. But with meditation, he found solace and solutions within himself. His actions grew less reactive and more mindful, as he explains to Dr. Rosenthal here (2016):

> I found that with meditation, my anxiety levels dropped considerably. It seems to me that the mind is fuel to the fire of fear. The mind can make us worry about things beyond their measure. And the great thing about meditation is that twice a day, the monkey mind just calms down. (para. 11)

It's clear that dedication to daily meditation has allowed Hugh Jackman and other notable names to find clarity and enrich their spiritual understanding of themselves. It has helped them improve their quality of life, embrace their busy work schedules, plan their social calendars, and build a healthy work–life balance.

The Long Game

When I read up on people truly imbibing the value of meditation, I find their transformation exhilarating. These people I have never met or spoken to have found similar clarity to what I have! They could be anyone—your average Joe, a high-flying businessman, Oprah Winfrey, Hugh Jackman, or the person standing just beside you who's engrossed in their cell phone.

We're in it for the long haul. I truly believe meditation and mindful exercises can benefit everyone who commits to them. Even if you find it challenging to quieten your mind, you will still notice a visible shift when your awareness grows larger and more focused. Soon, you will be able to set your phone aside and not be occupied by anything but the rhythm of your breathing.

With practice, you can develop a greater ability to remain present and sit in silence with nothing to distract you from yourself. It is a daunting task in today's noisy world, but it is possible and absolutely worth it. Remember, your spiritual journey isn't just about the destination. It's also about the commitment to nurturing your soul along the way. Embrace the process and let it transform you into someone who can appreciate the work it takes to be you every day of your life.

Expanding Your Spiritual Journey Beyond This Book

When it comes to exploring a world filled with stories of karma, reincarnation, and past lives, we need a little faith—faith in the universe, in our worth, and in the probability that there is meaning for those who choose to search. This faith is easier to hone when we practice expanding our spirituality and mindfulness. Seeking such experiences and teachings beyond the confines of a book can build your understanding and personal growth. When you find good connections with people on similar journeys, you enhance your learning through their insights.

Additional Sources

In fact, you will greatly benefit by stepping outside of traditional lessons and opening yourself up to the transformative experiences of everyday life. I've mentioned options for websites and organizations that provide access to sangha communities for this very reason. Embrace this opportunity to learn from others and expand your horizons!

Broaden your understanding of these topics by checking out the following:

Books

- *Karma: A Yogi's Guide to Crafting Your Destiny* (2021) by Sadhguru

- *The Gordian Knot of Self-Effort and Destiny* (2018) by Swami Advayananda

- *The Book of Joy: Lasting Happiness in a Changing World* (2016) by the 14th Dalai Lama, Desmond Tutu, and Douglas Abrams

- *The Power of Karma: How to Understand Your Past*

and Shape Your Future (2002) by Mary T. Browne

Podcasts

- *Tara Brach* by Tara Brach (https://www.tarabrach.com/talks-audio-video/)

- *Satsang With Shambhavi* by Shambhavi and Jaya Kula (https://jayakula.org/podcasts/)

- *On Purpose* by Jay Shetty (https://www.jayshetty.me/podcast)

- *Ghost Helpers* by Laura Van Tyne and Tina Erwin (https://thekarmicpath.libsyn.com/)

Online Courses

- Stanford University (https://www.classcentral.com/classroom/youtube-stanford-hospital-s-reverend-susan-scott-discusses-spirituality-and-aging-grief-and-loss-230072)

- Indica (https://indica.courses/enroll/cohort/introduction-to-the-law-of-karma/)

- Karma Lessons (https://www.karmalessons.com/)

Find recommended reading lists by well-known and certified therapists. The best way to find a spiritual connection to your true self and within the community is to explore the world around you, reach out to people, and interact as much as possible. It takes time and effort, but it leads you to beautiful places within yourself.

Conclusion

If we get to live repeated lives, then perhaps we can make progress across lifetimes and become better people. –Jim Tucker

So, here we are, at the end of the stretch, having traveled across the world to return home with a lot of luggage. By now, you know that the real meaning of karma is more than a souvenir; it has been the essence of our journey.

Let's go over the fundamental ideas we covered in each chapter.

1. Karma can be understood as the law of cause and effect. Every action, thought, and intention has consequences across lifetimes, shaping our future lives.

2. Reincarnation is the cycle of birth, death, and rebirth: samsara. The soul continues its journey through multiple lifetimes, each one offering opportunities for growth, learning, and spiritual evolution. Once we learn everything that we can from all the

consequences of our actions, we can gain liberation, known as moksha.

3. Real-life stories of reincarnation are out there. It is up to us to keep the discussion going. Cases of children recalling detailed memories of past lives provide a lot of evidence that reincarnation may be a reality. Their stories are food for thought, showing how the soul continues to exist.

4. Understanding the link between karma and reincarnation leads to personal growth. These concepts work together to help the evolution of our souls, encouraging us to make conscious choices that build positive karmic outcomes.

5. Accepting that some stories have holes in them need not devalue other accounts of reincarnation. We can address skepticism and misunderstandings by having open discussions with people and allowing everyone to explain their side. Some narratives of past lives do not have enough evidence, while others have an abundance. We must consider everything we find to refine the process and search for more.

6. Understanding karma helps us embrace the role of meditation. Actively practicing mindfulness and engaging in meditation can help us identify and shift negative karmic patterns, fostering emotional heal-

ing and spiritual progress. We can also explore past lives to break negative patterns, as reflecting on them can provide insight into unresolved issues or karmic debts. This empowers us to interrupt harmful habits and create positive change in this lifetime.

7. We find expression and growth in community and shared exploration. Engaging with like-minded individuals through workshops or online forums can deepen our understanding of karma and reincarnation.

You and Me, We're the Same

Accounts of true past-life memories and experiences can be thrilling and breathtaking. These stories provide potent insight into the interconnectedness of life and the impact of our actions. Understanding karma and reincarnation can show us how colorful and complex everyone's lives are, just like ours.

With this thought in my mind, the term "stranger" loses all meaning. I might have been in your shoes once upon a time. In another life, I might have struggled with the issues you are facing now. You may have met the challenges that I'm working on right now. Are we not sisters for dealing with the same concerns? Are we not brothers-in-arms for rising to meet our problems head-on? We are the same, you and me. Our souls have crossed paths, I'm sure. Maybe everyone's souls have done so.

We might never know all the people we once were. I might have been a father, an aunt, a mother, a grandpa, an uncle, a niece, a nephew, a cousin, a sibling, or a great-grandmother. I might have remained unwed in one past lifetime and brought many children into the world in a different one. I might have been allergic to grapes in one life and been a sommelier in another. I might have painted a daring portrait a hundred years ago and might have bought that very painting in another life.

Perhaps I was a potter a few thousand years ago, a monarch's advisor, a fisherman, a dancer, a merchant, a scribe, an engineer, a soldier, a construction worker, or an archer. Maybe tomorrow I will see a guitarist play in the subway and wonder if I have ever played music for crowds. I might get coffee from a nearby café and imagine myself as a barista in another country at another time. Perhaps I have been in the shoes of a nomad, traveling to sell my wares, hoping winter does not set in too quickly. I can imagine such scenarios so clearly it feels like they could have happened.

The soul contains quite a lot of might if you ask me. Perhaps I will be reborn into someone who will find this book and purchase it, knowing that something in the words will make my soul feel as though it was written for me. What a trip that would be! What an incredible journey my soul can go on!

I invite you to take this moment and reflect on your own beliefs and experiences with karma and reincarnation. Now, consider how everyone with similar questions and doubts has embarked on a journey just like yours. Millions of us take long-winding paths and arrive at different sides of the same answer. Connecting with others can offer valuable insights, shared experiences, and a sense of community for your spiritual growth. I'd like to emphasize the real power that lies in co-operation and collaboration.

Engaging in thoughtful conversations with those who share similar beliefs can truly expand your understanding and provide insight where you need it. These discussions can also inspire new perspectives on your own path. Whether through online discussions or local groups, finding a supportive network can greatly improve your temperament and emotional health. This contributes to a stronger state of mindfulness, which in turn benefits your spiritual journey.

Homestretch

So, go ahead. Find more sources to uncover. Researching these ideas from various cultural perspectives, such as old texts from Buddhism, Hinduism, and other spiritual traditions, can give you a well-rounded understanding of what karma truly entails. Everyone's perspective contains something unique to consider. This is why I encourage you to have a conversation about this. Whether it is through personal reflections, questions, or experiences, you and I can foster a community of exploration and mutual growth. I look forward to hearing your thoughts and continuing this enlightening journey!

Let's close this book with a powerful thought from an anthology book of essays, *Karma: Rhythmic Return to Harmony* (1975): "Karma has given us back the actual consequences of our own actions. The way we live, our actions and thoughts, enter a continuous stream of causes that determine our lives. Nothing is lost" (Nicholson et al., 1975, p. 14).

My takeaway from the spiritual concepts of karma, reincarnation, and past lives is immeasurably worthwhile. Shirley Nicholson is right. *Nothing* is lost to us. Every action, idea, intention, and thought is carried over through lives, transported and transformed. In a way, it reminds me of the universal rules of matter. Matter cannot be created or destroyed. It can only change forms. I believe this is what deep spirituality and karma bring to the table. Your lives change forms and reflect specific points at different moments. Plainly speaking, you matter.

Share Your Thoughts

T hank you from the bottom of my heart for supporting my book. Your time and engagement mean so much to me. If you enjoyed the journey, I would greatly appreciate it if you could take a moment to leave a review.

Your honest feedback not only helps other readers discover the book but also makes a huge difference for independent authors like me. Reviews are incredibly valuable—they guide, inspire, and allow stories to reach more people.

To leave a review, go to your Order History, locate the book, and click "Write a Product Review." If you're in the US, you can also scan the QR code below.

Thank you for being a part of this journey. I truly look forward to hearing your thoughts.

With gratitude,

Joyce T.

Bonus Gift

As a modest gesture to express my gratitude, I'd like to offer you a complimentary copy of my previously published e-book:

Decoding the Mystery of Life After Life: Passage to the Beyond, Near-Death Experiences, and Unveiling of the Afterlife's Mysteries

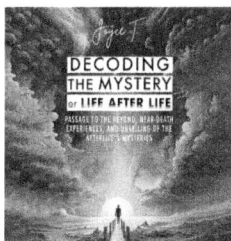

Access Code to Download the e-book: **life**

www.JoyceTbooks.com

References

Bering, J. (2013, November 2). Ian Stevenson's case for the afterlife: Are we "skeptics" really just cynics? *Scientific American.* https://www.scientificamerican.com/blog/bering-in-min d/ian-stevensone28099s-case-for-the-afterlife-are-we-e28 098skepticse28099-really-just-cynics/

Besant, A. (2012). *The theosophical writings of Annie Besant.* Jazzybee Verlag.

Bhagavati, M. J. S. (2011). *The 11 karmic spaces: Choosing freedom from the patterns that bind you.* Kashi Publishing.

Biblia. (n.d.). *Galatians 6:7–8.* https://biblia.com/bible/ niv/galatians/6/7-8

Bowman, C. [Carol Bowman Reincarnation]. (2021, Dec 10). *Carol Bowman and James Leininger, the boy who died in his past life as a WWII pilot, ABC Primetime* [Video]. YouTube. https://www.youtube.com/watch?v =QRefj5Mqg6U

Browne, M. T. (2003). *The power of karma: How to understand your past and shape your future.* Piatkus Books.

Cheryl [Handful of Leaves]. (2024, July 3). *Ep 47: Strength in the sangha: Growing together as a Buddhist community ft. Bro. Chye Chye* [Video]. YouTube. https://www.youtube.com/watch?v=odR7OKj0KAw

Cockell, J. (1993). *Yesterday's children: The extraordinary search for my past life family.* Piatkus.

David Lynch Foundation. (2023, June 7). *Selected research on transcendental mediation as a medical intervention for numerous physical and mental health conditions.* https://www.davidlynchfoundation.org/pdf/Research-on-TM.pdf

Dickens, C. (1863). *David Copperfield.* Bradbury Evans.

Haraldsson, E. (2017). Nazih Al-Danaf (reincarnation case). *Psi Encyclopedia.* London: The Society for Psychical Research. https://psi-encyclopedia.spr.ac.uk/articles/nazih-al-danaf-reincarnation-case

Haraldsson, E. & Matlock, J. G. (2017). *I saw a light and came here: Children's experiences of reincarnation.* White Crow Books.

Kleiman, D. (2024, August 10). *The unshakable beliefs that drive my healing practice.* Medium. https://medium.com/@DinaKleiman/the-unshakable-beliefs-that-drive-my-healing-practice-3380ff7a66d8

Lickerman, A. (2012, October 14). *The problem with reincarnation.* Psychology Today. https://www.psychologytoday.com/gb/blog/happiness-in-this-world/201210/the-problem-with-reincarnation

Luchte, J. (2012). *Pythagoras and the doctrine of transmigration: Wandering souls.* Continuum Publishing Corporation.

Moody, R. (2017). *Coming back: A psychiatrist explores past-life journeys.* CreateSpace Independent Publishing Platform.

Nicholson, S., Hanson, V., & Rosemarie Stewart, R. (Eds.). (1975). *Karma: Rhythmic return to harmony.* Quest Books.

Riley, A. (2021). How past lives affect our current life. *In My Sacred Space.* https://inmysacredspace.com/past-lives-affect-current-life/

Rohrbeck, J. [Thanatos TV]. (2017, October 5). *Past life memories, yesterday's children and reincarnation: An interview with Jenny Cockell* [Video]. YouTube. https://www.youtube.com/watch?v=GLkgr7mbP5o

Rosenthal, N. E. (2016). *How meditation changed Hugh Jackman's life.* Oprah. https://www.oprah.com/inspiration/how-meditation-changed-hugh-jackmans-life

Schechter, C. (2017). *Middah k'neged middah: Jewish "karma."* Sefaria. https://www.sefaria.org/sheets/79881?lang=bi

Silvestre, R. S. (2017). Karma theory, determinism, fatalism and freedom of will. *Logica Universalis, 11*(1), 1 0 . 1 0 0 7 / s 1 1 7 8 7 - 0 1 6 - 0 1 5 4 - z . https://www.researchgate.net/publication/306268382_Karma_Theory_Determinism_Fatalism_and_Freedom_of_Will

Stang, C. (2019, March 19). *Flesh and fire: Reincarnation and universal salvation in the early church.* Harvard Divinity S   c   h   o   o   l   . https://www.hds.harvard.edu/news/2019/03/19/flesh-and-fire-reincarnation-and-universal-salvation-early-church

Thich Nhat Hanh Foundation. (n.d.). Start a sangha. https://thichnhathanhfoundation.org/sangha-building-resources

Stevenson, I. (2000). *Children who remember previous lives: A question of reincarnation.* McFarland.

Thondup, T. (2006). *Peaceful death, joyful rebirth: A Tibetan Buddhist guidebook.* Shambhala Publications.

Travers, M. (2024, December 8). *A psychologist explains "past life memories"—and what they mean.* Forbes. https://www.forbes.com/sites/traversmark/2024/12/08/a-psychologist-explains-past-life-memories-and-what-they-mean/

Tucker, J. (2005). *Life before life: A scientific investigation of children's memories of previous lives.* St. Martin's Press.

Tutu, D. (2000). *No future without forgiveness.* Double-day.

Viereck, S., & Ford, H. (1928, August 26). Popular research topics: Henry Ford quotations [Interview]. *Detroit   Times.* https://www.thehenryford.org/collections-and-research/digital-resources/popular-topics/henry-ford-quotes/

Willard, A. K., Baimel, A., Turpin, H., Jong, J., & White-house, H. (2020). Rewarding the good and punishing the bad: The role of karma and afterlife beliefs in shaping moral norms. *Evolution and Human Behavior, 41*(5), 1090–5138. https://www.sciencedirect.com/science/article/pii/S1090513820300805

Image References

Abboud, L. (2024, March 2). Old photographs in a window [Image]. Pexels. https://www.pexels.com/photo/old-photographs-in-a-window-20479309/

Andrade, E. (2024, September 30). *Cozy coffee and gratitude journal on marble* [Image]. Pexels. https://www.pexels.com/photo/cozy-coffee-and-gratitude-journal-on-marble-28699940/

Beytlik. (2021, April 25). *Chess pieces placed on chessboard square* [Image]. Pexels. https://www.pexels.com/photo/chess-pieces-placed-on-chessboard-square-7644275/

CJ. (2024, February 13). *A large tree with a statue in the middle of it* [Image]. Unsplash. https://unsplash.com/photos/a-large-tree-with-a-statue-in-the-middle-of-it-uW7_j6JUQqY

Grabowska, K. (2015, May 17). *Old photos in the wooden box* [Image]. Pexels. https://www.pexels.com/photo/old-photos-in-the-wooden-box-5842/

İpek, A. (2024, August 28). *A woman is walking on the beach with a blurred image* [Image]. Pexels. https://www.pexels.com/photo/a-woman-is-walking-on-the-beach-with-a-blurred-image-28077293/

Pixabay. (2016, March 16). *Gray Newton's cradle in close-up photogaphy* [Image]. Pexels. https://www.pexels.com/photo/gray-newton-s-cradle-in-close-up-photogaphy-60582/

Shkraba, A. (2020, August 29). *Woman in white long sleeve shirt sitting beside woman in white long sleeve shirt* [Image]. Pexels. https://www.pexels.com/photo/woman-in-white-long-sleeve-shirt-sitting-beside-woman-in-white-long-sleeve-shirt-5217836/

Starostin, S. (2024, October 10). *Hexagonal shelves with inspirational decor* [Image]. Pexels. https://www.pexels.com/photo/hexagonal-shelves-with-inspirational-decor-28865900/

Thirdman. (2021, February 26). *A woman sitting on ham-mock* [Image]. Pexels. https://www.pexels.com/photo/a-woman-sitting-on-hammock-6958591/

Printed in Dunstable, United Kingdom

71826288R00109